DIAMOND & BOSS
A HOOD LOVE STORY

DANI LITTLEPAGE

Diamond & Boss: A Hood Love Story

Copyright © 2019 by Dani Littlepage

All rights reserved.

Published in the United States of America.

All rights reserved. No part of this publication may be reproduced, distributed, or transmitted in any form or by any means, including photocopying, recording, or other electronic or mechanical methods, without the prior written permission of the publisher, except in the case of brief quotations embodied in critical reviews and certain other noncommercial uses permitted by copyright law. For permission requests, please contact: www.colehartsignature.com

This is a work of fiction. Names, characters, places, and incidents either are the products of the author's imagination or are used fictitiously. Any resemblance of actual persons, living or dead, businesses, companies, events, or locales is entirely coincidental. The publisher does not have any control and does not assume any responsibility for author or third-party websites or their content.

The unauthorized reproduction or distribution of this copyrighted work is a crime punishable by law. No part of the book may be scanned, uploaded to or downloaded from file sharing sites, or distributed in any other way via the Internet or any other means, electronic, or print, without the publisher's permission. Criminal copyright infringement, including infringement without monetary gain, is investigated by the FBI and is punishable by up to five years in federal prison and a fine of $250,000 (www.fbi.gov/ipr/).

This book is licensed for your personal enjoyment only. Thank you for respecting the author's work.

Published by Cole Hart Signature, LLC.

Mailing List

To stay up to date on new releases, plus get information on contests, sneak peeks, and more,

Go To The Website Below...

WWW.COLEHARTSIGNATURE.COM

❀ Created with Vellum

CHAPTER 1

"Damn, lil mama! Shake that shit!" Quentin slapped the ass of the stripper that was giving him a lap dance.

Obeying his command, the stripper bent over so he could get a better view of her pussy as she grabbed her ankles, and continued to shake her fat, round ass. Quentin tossed twenties and fifties on the stripper as he drank Hennessey straight from the bottle. He briefly took his eyes off the stripper's body to scan the room. He nodded his head in approval when he saw that his team was enjoying themselves just as much as he was. The private mansion party that Quentin surprised his employees with was a celebration for their hard work in the launch of his sixth business.

Quentin always rewarded his employees in one way or another. Whether it was cash or parties, he believed that if he did right by his employees, they would remain loyal, and do right by him in return. After being an entrepreneur for nearly a decade, his theory remained true.

"Aye, Boss! I see you over there, man!" His right hand man

and business partner, Bashir a.k.a Banks, shouted over the loud music. "Shorty shaking that shit like she tryna fuck or something," he laughed.

"She keep it up, I might just have to give her this D later," Quentin gave Bashir a pound.

"Take a break for a minute, man. I need to holla at you about something."

"Aight," Quentin stood up from his seat.

Whispering something in the stripper's ear, the two men headed upstairs away from the noise. Once they were inside the office, Quentin flipped the switch before closing the door behind him. Taking a seat behind the desk, Bashir removed the blunt from his ear and lit it.

"What's on your mind, Banks?"

"I just wanted you to know that I appreciate you for allowing me to be your business partner for the past two years, man." Banks exhaled the weed smoke. "There were niggas in ya ear telling you not to take a chance on me, but you ignored them haters, and for that, I'm forever grateful my nigga." He passed the blunt to Quentin.

"Nigga, you pulled me away from a bomb ass party so we can have a heart to heart?" Quentin laughed.

"Come on, man. Stop clowning," Bashir chuckled.

"Aight man but on a serious note, I'm glad you feel that way because I decided to let you run the new business we just launched." Quentin's tone turned serious before hitting the blunt.

"Stop bullshitting me, Boss," he replied in disbelief.

"Real talk," he choked on the smoke before exhaling. "You've done well under my supervision for the past couple of years, and the way you've stepped up to the plate when the barbershop was broken into last year, showed me that you can handle shit on ya own. So, with the launch of our newest business venture, I'm gonna let you run the show my nigga."

"That's what the fuck I'm talking about, Boss," Bashir shouted as he jumped up from the chair. "Thanks for this opportunity, man. You know you can count on me to get this shit popping," he clapped his hands together.

"I know. Just don't let this shit go to ya head and start acting brand new and shit. You know how I operate, and how I conduct business. Yeah, the club is your responsibility, but remember that both of our names is on this shit. You feel me?" He stated sternly, rising up from the chair.

"I got you homie, and I give you my word that you ain't got shit to worry about," Bashir reassured him.

The two men shook hands before finishing the blunt and heading back to the party where a small crowd of women were gathered in the middle of the floor. The duo rushed over to see what was going on, and when Quentin saw Kamaya, his go to girl, and the stripper that was giving him a lap dance, in the middle of the crowd about to exchange blows, he snatched Kamaya away from the thick red bone and pulled her into the bathroom.

"What the fuck are you doing here, Kamaya?" He roared. "I didn't invite you here!"

"I know you didn't invite me here and I can see why. I heard you were having the time of ya life with that ho's ass all in ya face," she rolled her neck. "I bet you were gonna fuck that bitch. Weren't you?"

"And if I wanted to, what concern is it of yours? You're not my fucking girl, Kamaya. I keep telling ya ass that. Yes, you're my go to bitch when I need an escort for a date, sexual favors and when I need strippers for my events, but that's it. You keep getting beside ya'self tryna check the bitches that I interact with. You keep this shit up, I'm gonna cut ya ass off altogether. Do you understand me?" Quentin spoke through gritted teeth.

Kamaya stared at him without responding.

"I said do you understand me," he stepped closer to her.

"Yeah," she frowned.

"Now, get the fuck outta here and I don't wanna see or hear from you until I need you."

Snatching the bathroom door open, Kamaya stormed out towards the front door with Quentin on her heels. She opened the front door letting herself out and he slammed it closed behind her. He gave instructions to his security not to let her back in before going back into the bathroom and taking a moment to get himself together. Taking a few deep breaths, Boss thought about Kamaya and the stunt she'd just pulled. It was the third one in the past month and a half, and the shit was starting to annoy him. Their three-year business relationship went from sugar to shit when Kamaya popped up on him in a business meeting, confronting him about a young woman he had dinner with. When Boss explained that the woman was his cousin that was visiting from out of town, Kamaya had to pay for her actions with ass kissing and being an errand girl for Boss. Although he warned her to cool out with the bullshit, she still took it upon herself to try him. Quentin felt like it might be time for them to part ways, but he never had the courage to cut her off.

Besides the ratchetness, Kamaya was an important asset to his business. He brought her along when it was time for him to close business deals, and Kamaya was always his escort to black tie affairs. She even recruited strippers and waitresses for his private parties. Not to mention, her sex game was nothing short of amazing. Quentin felt like he would suffer a major loss if he let Kamaya go. So, he decided to put up with her and her nonsense a little while longer.

Returning to the party, Quentin grabbed another bottle of Henny before strolling over to the thick red bone that was waiting for him. She pushed him down in the chair and continued her lap dance. He took a huge swig from the bottle putting the situation with Kamaya to the back of his mind for the moment. All Quentin wanted to do was enjoy the rest of the party and finish the night with a bang. With the help of the fine ass stripper, he knew it was going to be worth his time and money.

CHAPTER 2

"What the fuck you mean you have to cancel? Do you know how long it took me to set this fucking date up, Diamond?"

"Jordan, I'm giving you more than enough notice, okay? I told you I have to go over my research paper before I submit it to my professor, and on top of that, you know I have to take care of my brother," Diamond explained to her bestie. "Besides, you know how I feel about dating. I'm done with that."

"Girl, do you hear yourself right now? Your only twenty-five, Diamond, and you're talking about you're done with dating. I know losing your fiancé was tragic, but I'm sure he wouldn't want you putting your life on hold like this. You gotta find the strength to move on," Jordan spoke sincerely.

Hearing her best friend speak about her ex broke her heart and brung tears to her eyes. Every time her ex was mentioned, it brought back the pain that she'd been trying to bury for the past three years. The day she graduated from college, the love of her life, Damien, proposed to her in front of her entire graduating class. Receiving her degree, along with the proposal from the man she loved most, overwhelmed her with joy. Diamond was looking forward to spending the rest of her life with Damien. He was the only man she saw herself being with. She was ready for a life filled with love, happiness, and kids, but a car accident caused by a drunk driver killed him and Diamond's dream. People close to her tried to convince her that she should move on with her life, but to Diamond, it was easier said than done. The love she had for Damien ran too deep for her to just forget about him and move on; but nobody seemed to understand that.

"Diamond? You still there?" Jordan called out to her.

"Yeah. I'm here," she answered sadly.

"Look, girl. I didn't mean to make you sad. It's just that you're my girl, and I just wanna see you happy."

"I know you do Jay, and I will be. Have fun on your date and give me all the details," Diamond forced a smile.

"Aight," she sighed. "Tell lil bro I said wassup and good luck on your paper, even though you're a damn genius."

"Thanks girl," she chuckled. "Talk to you later."

Ending the call, Diamond returned her focus to her MacBook Pro. The conversation she had with Jordan lingered in her thoughts before sheput the finishing touches on her research paper. After proofreading it, she printed her paper before placing it in her folder. Her assignment wasn't due until the end of the week, but she needed to get it out the way so she could study for an upcoming exam. Glancing at the clock on the wall, Diamond slipped her feet into her Ugg boots before putting on her coat. She snatched up her phone, keys and wallet, then headed out the door. The winter air smacked her in the face as she walked out of her apartment building.

Power walking to her 2017 silver Honda Accord, Diamond popped the locks with the remote and hopped inside, quickly shutting the door behind her. Winters in Philly were brutal. Besides the below freezing temperatures, the snow storms that accumulated more than a foot of snow was more than enough to make any person want to stay in the house, but the cold weather and snow never stopped people from making it to their daily hustle if they needed to be there. Revving the engine, Diamond let her car warm up for a few minutes before cruising out of the lot and into traffic.

She arrived at the Shane Victorino Boys and Girls Club in the Nicetown section of Philly twenty-five minutes later and hopped out the car, leaving it running. Normally, leaving her car running was something she never did due to the fact that that was an easy way for niggas to steal her shit, but since she was familiar with the people in the neighborhood, Diamond was cool leaving her car unattended. To be on the safe side, she paid a few kids that were coming out of the club a few dollars to watch it. Walking inside, Diamond was about to ask for the receptionist to page her brother, until he came strolling down the stairs.

"Wassup D," Justin greeted her with a hug.

"Hey baby bro. Well don't you look handsome with ya fresh haircut." She ran her hand over Justin's low-cut fade, making him blush.

"You know it runs in the family," he replied cockily.

"Come on boy," Diamond chuckled pushing him towards the door.

Thanking the kids for watching her car, she watched how her brother eyed a group of girls that were walking by.

"Hey Justin," a pretty brown skin girl spoke.

"Hey Kailyn," he smirked.

The girls giggled as they continued walking by. Diamond shook her head at her brother as they hopped in the car. Pulling off down the street, she noticed Justin almost broke his neck to get another glimpse of the of Kailyn as they drove by.

"Damn lil bro. You like her like that?" She teased getting her brothers attention.

"I don't know what you talking 'bout, sis," he chuckled.

"Boy, please. Don't no man break their neck to look at no female unless he's interested. So stop fronting and spill the beans, boy."

Justin ran his hand over his face before responding.

"Kailyn and I have a few classes together and we partnered up on a few projects. She's really smart, and I find myself daydreaming about her sometimes, but—"

"But what?"

"I think she has a dude already, and I have a girl," Justin solemnly answered.

"You mean that ratchet from 17th and Erie? What's her name? Uhhh—"

"Tisha."

"I can't believe you still talk to her, Justin. You know you can do so much better than that, but just like the rest of these niggas, you got a thing for these hood bitches," Diamond shook her head in disgust.

"Good girls are boring, D. The always play by the rules and they're too scared to take risk. Hood girls are down for whatever, and are freaks in the bedroom," Justin nodded his head.

"And how the hell would you know that?" Diamond glanced at him as they approached a red light.

Justin shifted in his seat before looking out the window.

"Oh my God! Justin!" she shouted. "When the fuck did you start having sex?"

"In November over Thanksgiving Break….at the house."

"In my damn house! Jesus take the wheel!" she shouted

clutching her necklace. "Have you been using protection, Justin?"

"No. I've just been pulling out. Tisha said we don't need to use condoms because we're only sleeping with each other," he shrugged.

"You damn dummy! You're still supposed to use protection! Pulling out ain't gonna stop that lil heffa from getting pregnant or prevent you from getting an STD! You need to start thinking for yourself, boy. If you're gonna be out here fucking, ya ass need to strap the fuck up. These girls out here are nasty, and you need to be careful. Do you hear me?"

"Yes sis," he mumbled.

The car fell silent for a moment before Justin spoke again.

"Just to let you know, me and Tisha ain't rocking like that no more. I found out she was cheating on me with some dude on the football team. So, I cut her off, but she keeps trying to get back with me."

"Leave her lil fast ass alone, bro. She's not for you. You need to be with someone that's about something like you are. You get straight A's and you're the captain of the debate team. You have a lot going for yourself, and you don't need nothing or no one fucking up your future, aight?"

Justin nodded his head in agreement.

Diamond stopped by the Save-A-Lot in the Germantown section of Philly to do some grocery shopping, before heading to their apartment in the Ivy Hill. As she put the food away, Diamond noticed the family photo they took with their mother when she was ten, and her brother was a baby. Diamond smiled at the picture before continuing to put the food away Only keeping out what she wanted to cook. Glancing over at her brother who was sitting at the dining room table doing his homework, it was still hard for her to believe that their mother abandoned them five years ago for the so-called man of her dreams, Making Diamond become the guardian of her fifteen-year-old brother.

Their mother, Tabitha, was always head over heels for a man, but she never left them for one. The text message Tabitha sent them was short and sweet: *"I dedicated my life to y'all. Now it's time I have a life of my own. Take care of each other. I love y'all."* From that day forward, they looked out for each other.

On top of her taking care of her brother, Diamond attended night classes at La'Salle University while managing a career as an Operations Manager in the Human Resources Department for the City of Philadelphia, which she was obtaining her master's degree for. Learning that her brother was sexually active was something that Diamond wasn't prepared for. She knew that the day would come, but she thought that her mother would be around to handle it. Since it was up to her now, Diamond prayed that she had what it took to raise Justin the right way

CHAPTER 3

After depositing the money for his businesses in the bank early Tuesday morning, Quentin strolled to his car as his phone began to ring for the fifth time. Knowing that it was Kamaya calling, he silenced the ringing purposely, letting the call go to voicemail. He knew how much she hated it when he didn't answer her calls, but this was all part of her punishment for the stunt she pulled at the party on Saturday. Hopping into his black 2018 Yukon Denali, Quentin's phone connected to the car and Meek Mill's 'Going Bad' featuring Drake began to play as he pulled into traffic, making his way downtown to his office.

Quentin pulled into his parking spot in the underground garage a half hour later before killing the engine. Securing the locks on truck, he stepped on the elevator, rode it to the top floor and strolled down the hall. The smell of his Polo cologne brought on lustful stares from his female employees, which caused him to smile as they flirtatiously said good morning while Quentin walked past. Standing at 6'3", he bared the resemblance to Rick Ross, but not as heavy. His mustache and beard were neatly trimmed and he was rocking a low cut with waves. Quentin didn't think he was much of a looker, but whenever he put on a suit, like the navy-blue Armani one he was rocking, it made him feel like he was the sexiest nigga on earth.

Heading to his office, Quentin opened the door and was met with an outburst from Kamaya.

"You got some nerve having me wait here for two damn hours," she jumped up from the chair.

"After the stunt you pulled over the weekend, ya ass is lucky I'm even talking to you at all," Quentin brushed past her.

"If ya ass wasn't fucking everything walking, I wouldn't act the way I do, Quentin," she crossed her arms over her chest.

"And why the fuck is that any of your concern, Kamaya? Because if memory serves me correctly, we are not a couple. We work together. That's all."

"And I need to be more than just your damn partner. You have me involved in damn near every part of your life but you won't make me your girl, and I don't understand why," she stepped closer to him.

"Maya," he sighed, "You already know I would rather not talk about this, because my response is only gonna hurt you. I told you when we crossed the line and became physical that I shoulda ended things with you, and the only reason I didn't was because you promised me that you could keep ya feelings and emotions intact, but you lied."

Kamaya's eyes quickly shifted to the floor then back to Quentin's.

"Look, I need to know if you're gonna be cool with our arrangement because the next time you decide to roll up on any chick that I deal with outside of you, I'm cutting you off completely," Quentin stated sternly. "So, is this gonna be a problem, Kamaya?"

"No, it's not."

"Good. Now, don't call or text me for the next two weeks and when I need you, I'll call you. Have a good day," he politely dismissed her.

With her mouth hitting the floor, Kamaya turned on her heels and headed out of the office. Quentin's eyes stayed glued on her round ass until the door slammed shut behind her. The charcoal pants suit she was wearing hugged her thick frame which made his dick hard. If they were on good terms, Quentin would've blessed her with some dick, but since she was on punishment, he was going to have to find someone else to fulfill his sexual desires.

After taking a few minutes to clear his head, Quentin took a seat at hit large desk then powered up the multiple computer monitors that were placed on his desk. Each monitor displayed the cameras that were placed in each of his establishments. He had a breakfast shop in Roxborough, a barbershop in Logan, a clothing store in Mt. Airy, a hair/nail salon in West Oakland, and a seafood restaurant in Center City along with the new club. The barbershop and the hair salon were the first businesses Quentin opened, and although the two businesses suffered a few losses over the years, they were the most successful out of all of his establishments.

He watched the monitors closely for nearly two hours to make sure things were running smoothly, and that his staff was acting accordingly. Besides the club, the breakfast shop was his newest operation which meant that he had to keep a close eye on it. Although Quentin had employees there he could trust, that didn't stop him from making surprise monthly visits just to see how things were going, and to communicate directly with his employees. The one-year anniversary of the breakfast shop was a few months away and even thought things were operating smoothly, Quentin felt that the shop still needed grooming. Opening his Macbook Pro, he pulled up Google and searched for ways to improve the shop and training courses for his employees.

As he jotted notes down on his notepad, his phone began to ring and by the song that was playing, he knew it was his little cousin, Niko, calling.

"Yo, lil cuz. What it is?" Quentin greeted with a smile.

"Nothing much, man. Just the usual. School, football, parties and girls," Niko chuckled. "But since the season is over, I've just been chilling man."

"That's wassup. So, what's on your mind? I can tell by the tone of your voice something is wrong," he leaned forward on his desk.

"I need you to rescue me, man. My mom caught me fucking my girl in her bed yesterday, and she damn near killed my ass. I need ya help, cuz."

"What the fuck? Hold up. Aunt Kim don't get off work until like eight at night. You mean to tell me you couldn't get rid of your girl by then?"

"My girl leaves my crib at five so she can beat her mom home, but my mom came home for something and caught us getting it in. I was just about to nut and when I saw my mom, my shit instantly got soft. She told us to get dressed, told my girl to leave and as soon as she was out the door, she fucked me up, Q. My mom was fighting me like I was nigga in the street! Not only did she whoop my ass but she put me on punishment for a month. She took my PS4 and everything. I can't do shit man."

Quentin burst into laughter.

"Come on, cuz. This shit ain't funny man," Niko whined. "You gotta help me."

"I'm sorry. I'm sorry," Quentin ceased his laughter. "Aight. I'm not gonna lie and say that you didn't buy that ass whooping and punishment, but you ain't the first lil nigga to get caught fucking in their parents' bed, and you definitely won't be the last. As far as me helping you, I guess I could convince your mom to allow you to come work for me on the weekends at one of my spots and stay with me. How does that sound?"

"I don't mind staying over your crib every weekend and as far as me working, am I gonna get paid?" Niko inquired.

"Come on now. Why would I have you work for me and not pay you? What part of the game is that?"

"I just had to make sure. How much are we talking?"

"We'll discuss that after I talk to aunt Kim. I like to discuss business of any kind in person, so I can read people to see if they're bullshitting me. Once I get ya moms on board, I'll let you know where to meet me at. If all goes right, you'll be starting this Friday after school. Aight?"

"That's good enough for me. Thanks, cuz."

"No problem, Niko."

"Aye. Is it cool if I bring one of my homies with me? He's looking for work so he can help his sister with bills and shit."

"Ya homie don't stay with his mom?"

"Nah. His mom dipped on him when he was ten and his sister been taking care of him since then. She works in the day time and goes to school at night. He said that she's holding shit down for them, but he wants to help her out," Niko explain.

"He sounds like a stand-up dude. Not ignorant like the rest of the lil niggas you roll with."

"Yeah. Justin is different. He's not into all that hood shit. He tries to keep me outta trouble. So, I've been trying to take a page outta his book so I can be college bound and shit."

"I can't believe my ears. If this dude got you trying to walk the straight and narrow, I definitely need to meet him. So, yeah. If things work out with ya mom, you can bring him with you and he can stay the weekend, too."

"Cool. Thanks again, man. Let me know what she says."

Ending the call with his cousin, Quentin chuckled to himself as he replayed their conversation. He recalled a few times where he had almost gotten caught when he was sneaking around and fucking girls in the crib as a teen as well, but unlike his little cousin, Quentin never got caught. Thinking about how fast Niko was growing up and the stupid shit he got in to every now and then, Q felt like it was time for him to step up and take Niko under his wing. His aunt was raising him as a single parent and he could imagine how challenging it was for her raising a young man without a father. Even though he didn't view himself as a role model, Quentin believed that he could make a difference in his cousin's life.

Around two in the afternoon, Q completed his work goals for the day and shut everything down in his office before leaving out. He gave his secretary a short list of things to do then headed towards the elevator, barley making it in time before the doors closed. Arriving at the first floor, Quentin stepped off, strolled through the lobby out the front door of the building. Unbothered by the freezing January weather, he walked the short distance to the Capital Grille that was a few feet away. Entering the restaurant, Quentin greeted the hostess and she quickly escorted him to a table. As he slid in the booth, the hostess placed the menu down in front of him, told him his server would be with him shortly with a seductive smile, and walked off. Picking up the menu, Quentin took his time deciding what he wanted to eat. Once he made a decision, he place his menu to the side and spotted two beautiful women that were sitting a few tables away from him. He watched the women as they engaged in conversation, and Q was blown away by the brown skinned woman's bright smile. When his waiter approached his table, he gave him his food and drink order. After the waiter recited it back to him, Quentin pulled out of his pocket and wrote something on a napkin.

"Aye, can you do me a favor? Can you give this to the ladies sitting at that table over there?" Q nodded.

"Sure," the waiter responded, taking the napkin out of Q's hand.

He watched the waiter as he approached the table and as he handed one of the women the napkin. They looked in his direction and Quentin waved at them. One of the women waved back while the other rolled her eyes. He watched as they read the note of him offering to pay for their lunch. They both looked in his direction before they wrote something down on the napkin, handing it back to the waiter. Returning to Quentin, the waiter handed him the napkin before walking away.

Opening it, he chuckled when he read *'no'*, followed by an exclamation point. No woman had ever turned him down when he offered them anything, and he wasn't sure how he felt about their response. Glancing in their direction, he saw that the women were gathering their things to leave. As they headed towards his direction, Quentin scanned their bodies with his eyes. One of the women kept walking while the other one stopped at his table.

"How about I pay for your lunch," the brown skinned woman smirked, dropping some money on the table before walking off.

Quentin unfolded the money and was taken aback by the three C notes he counted. He turned around to see if the woman was still in the restaurant, but she had left. Still stunned, he placed the money in his jacket pocket as the waiter placed his drink and appetizer on the table. Taking a sip of his Henny, Q's mind was racing a mile a minute as he thought about the brown skinned beauty and her gesture. The fact that she turned him down and gave him three hundred dollars for his lunch had his mind blown. Not only was the woman beautiful, but she showed him that she was also independent and didn't need a man to take care of her. The impression that she left him had Quentin ready to hunt her down and return her money, but he figured he'd hold onto it, and return it when he saw her again.

CHAPTER 4

After leaving Quentin's office, Kamaya went to the hair salon spending the majority of her day locked in her office. The conversation she had with Boss that morning had her blood pressure through the roof and her feelings hurt. She knew that he was going to be pissed at her for crashing his party, but for Boss to dismiss her the way he did and telling her not to contact him for two weeks, was going overboard to her. Kamaya couldn't believe that he could treat her as if she was just some random bitch instead of his companion and business partner. For the past three years, she had helped Boss take his businesses to the next level as well as his status as an entrepreneur. Whenever it was time for him to seal a business deal, he always brought her along. Not only to compliment him and distract his opposition, but as a back up just in case his original business approach didn't work. With a master's degree in business, Kamaya knew how to work every angle to her advantage, so they could come out on top and they always did. Her beauty and brains combo were something to be fucked with, and for

Boss to not treat her or view her as his equal, messed with her mentally.

When they crossed the line and became intimate nearly a year ago, Kamaya convinced herself that she would be able to keep her feelings under control so they could maintain their healthy partnership, but every time they fucked or spent quality time together, her feelings increased for Boss. Being the confident, independent and strong woman that she was, Kamaya was certain that she was the only woman that he was fucking and spending time with, but when she discovered that he was fucking other females, it shattered her ego and caused her to be the one thing she never was. Jealous. Whenever Kamaya heard or saw Boss with another bitch, her anger became unbearable and the hurt only added to her rage. She knew that they weren't officially a couple, but the way she felt about him wouldn't allow her to accept that. She couldn't handle seeing him with other woman, and the thought of him fucking another bitch damn near drove her crazy. Kamaya believed that her and Boss were meant to be together. Besides their dynamic work chemistry, the bond that they developed over the years seemed unbreakable. She told him things about herself that she never shared with anyone. Not even her best friend. Kamaya felt safe and secure whenever she was in his presence, and the fact that she could talk to him about anything without judgement on his end, made things that much better. Although she had niggas begging her to give them a chance, Kamaya only had eyes for Boss. She wanted to be his girl, and she was willing to make that happen by any means.

As quitting time approached, Kamaya shut down her laptop and secured her office. She made sure everything was turned off before locking the front door of the salon. She popped the locks to her 2018 pearl blue Lexus Coupe, tossed her purse and coat in the passenger seat, then took her place behind the wheel, slamming the door shut. Bringing the car to life, Kamaya pulled into traffic and headed to the expressway. When Amerie's 'Why Don't We Fall In Love' came on, she turned up the volume and nodded her head to the music, with thoughts of Boss on her mind. Arriving at her condo complex twenty minutes later, Kamaya parked in her spot killing the engine. She grabbed her things and locked the doors to her car before power walking into her building. Kamaya waved to the doorman as she made her way to the elevator. Riding it to the second floor, she stepped off heading down the hall. When she heard Trina's classic 'The Baddest Bitch' coming from inside, Kamaya knew her friend and roommate, Ebony, was in her bag about something. Unlocking the door, she shook her head when she saw her friend standing in front of the mirror, rapping the lyrics to the song. Kamaya closed the door behind her before walking over to the Beats Pill Speaker, turning the volume down.

"Bout time ya ass got home, Maya," she shouted. "I need to vent. I got L's rolled and Apple E&J waiting for us."

"So do I. Let me change my clothes and I'll meet you out there."

"Cool."

Kamaya strolled down the hall to her bedroom, tossing her things onto her California king size bed. Kicking off her Christian Louboutin's heels, she stripped down to her underwear before grabbing a tank top and a pair of biker shorts from her dresser and putting them on. Kamaya retrieved her phone from her purse then headed back to the living room where Ebony already started smoking.

"Aight Ebo. What's going on?" Kamaya asked, joining her friend on the couch.

"This nigga Ramon got me fucked all the way up sis," she exhaled the weed smoke. "Tell me how I go to meet this nigga for lunch today and he drops a bomb on me."

"What bomb?"

"That he's getting married next month, and his soon to be wife is expecting their second child!"

"Get the fuck outta here!" Kamaya jumped up from the couch. "You've been with that nigga for two years. Where the fuck did shawty and the kids come from?"

"He told me that he'd been with her for four years and that they share a home together in Delaware. He said that he wasn't expecting things to get so serious between us because we were only fuck buddies at first, but he ended up catching feelings for me and that's why he stayed with me," Ebony passed her the blunt. "When Ramon told me that he was cutting me off so he could be faithful to his fiancée, I tossed my drink in his face and dumped my plate of food in his lap. I told him to suck a sick dick and die before I left."

"Damn, Ebony. I'm so sorry. I know how much you loved Ramon." Kamaya placed a hand on her friend's shoulder while she hit the blunt.

"You don't know how fucking stupid I feel, Maya. Normally, I woulda seen some type of sign that he wasn't being true to me, but I don't know if the signs were there all along and I missed them, or if that nigga was really that damn slick with his shit."

"Maybe you saw the signs or felt that something wasn't right but chose to ignore them because of how much you loved him. You know how being in love can be, Ebony. We be blinded by that shit," She exhaled the weed smoke, passing the blunt back to her bestie.

"You ain't never lied about that shit. I can't believe that nigga played me like this," Ebony chuckled. "I'm cool on this love shit, Maya. I'm tired of being played and hurt. This shit is for the birds, man."

"I know how you feel. I'm starting to feel the same the way."

"What the fuck happened between you and Boss now?"

"I told you I popped up at his mansion party over the weekend."

"Yeah, and he kicked ya ass out."

"Okay. So this nigga texts me this morning telling me to meet him in his office by eight. Boss doesn't show up until 10:15am."

"That bastard kept you waiting for two fucking hours?"

"Yes, girl! So, I said something to him about him fucking other females and he said that's none of my concern because we're not a couple. I told him that I should be more than just his business partner and I didn't understand why he wouldn't make me his girl. His response was that he didn't like talking about that because I was going to be hurt by his answer. Boss told me in order for us to continue with our relationship, I was gonna have to control my emotions. After I agreed to do so, he dismissed me and told me not to contact him for two weeks," Maya removed the cap from the E&J filling her cup.

"That son of bitch got some nerve! How the fuck can he treat you like that after all the shit you've done for him and his business? I warned you about getting sexually involved with that nigga, but ya ass wouldn't listen," Ebony passed Maya the L then lit another one.

"I don't need the 'I told you so' speech, okay? I just need your advice on how to make him my man."

"Bitch, are you dumb? The man clearly doesn't want a relationship with you, but ya ass still wants to be with him? Don't get me wrong. Boss is one hell of a catch. He's handsome, a successful business man, bu-coo amount of money and from what you told me, his sex game is amazing. I just feel like you're just gonna end up getting even more than you already are if you keep trying to complete this mission of making him your man, sis," she expressed with sincerity.

"I hear what you're saying, Ebony, but I believe if I stick with him, not bitch about him being with other women and keep my feelings in check, he'll see that I'm the woman for him."

"If you're gung-ho on making this nigga ya man, I can't stop you. Just don't say I didn't try to warn you. My only advice is do you. Don't wait on that nigga to come around. Go on dates and have fun until he does." Ebo filled her cup with the brown liquid then took a sip.

"That doesn't sound like a bad idea," Kamaya finished the blunt.

The ladies sat in silence as they continued to drink and smoke. Sade's 'Smooth Operator' played softly in the background as Maya thought about Boss and her mission. Mentally putting a plan into motion, she decided to pull out all the stops and step out of her comfort zone. In her twenty-nine years on earth, she never had to work hard for any man that she wanted. Men usually had to jump through hoops just to get a date with her, and now that she was considering doing the same for Boss, made her briefly question herself. There was no doubt that he was worth all the things Kamaya had planned on doing, but thoughts of her going out of her way for this man just for him to still not want her, was a thought she couldn't fathom. Instead of letting the negativity linger, she chose to go through with her plan because she didn't intend to fail. Once she proved to Boss that she was all the woman he needed, he would have no choice but to make her his woman. Maybe his wife.

CHAPTER 5

When Friday rolled around, Diamond had a good mind to take a sick day from work. After spending most of her time studying for her exams and attending class the night before, the last thing she wanted to do was get her ass up for work that morning but calling out wasn't an option. Grabbing her phone off the night stand, Diamond checked her account to see if her direct deposit hit and when she saw the amount, she found the energy to get herself up out of bed. The extra hours she put in made a difference in her check and motivated her to do it as often as she could. Besides the bills she had to pay, Diamond needed the extra money to take care of her and Justin, who seemed to be growing daily. Between haircuts, his monthly transpass for the bus, clothes, sneakers for his size ten feet, his weekend activities and not to mention the money she spent on herself, the extra funds were desperately needed.

When Diamond got custody of Justin, taking care of him wasn't a problem, but when he hit eighth grade, everything began to change. She wasn't aware of the change's boys went through when they hit puberty. So, to watch him transform into a young man right before her eyes damn near drove her crazy, but it wasn't as bad as she thought it would be.

Jumping out of bed, Diamond made her way to the bathroom to get fresh for the day. When she was finished taking care of her hygiene, she headed back to her room and picked out her outfit, placing it on the bed. Diamond grabbed her black lace Victoria's Secret underwear from her dresser and put them on. After applying her 'A Thousand Wishes' lotion to her body, she put on her red Polo button up shirt and a pair of light denim Old Navy jeans with a pair of red Coach flats. Tucking her shirt in, Diamond put on her red Coach belt that matched her shoes before walking over to her vanity to do her hair and make-up.

When she was finished, Diamond went over to her full-length mirror check herself out. Her 5' 6" frame was tiny, but her titties and ass were far from it. Her 36C boobs, apple bottom ass and pretty face caught the attention of any man. The hating bitches in her building swore that her titties and ass were fake, but she was all natural. The only thing that was fake on her was the short bob she was rocking and her stiletto nails. Nodding her head in approval, Diamond grabbed her denim blazer from her closet along with her red Coach purse. She filled it with everything she needed before saying bye to her brother who was just getting out of bed. She snatched her coat off the rack on her way out the door, closing it behind her.

As she left her building, Diamond unlocked the doors to her car when her phone began to ring. The tone that was playing let her know it was Jordan calling. When she was settled inside her car, she retrieved her phone from the bag and quickly answered.

"Hey, Jay. What's going on?" She placed the keys in the ignition starting the car.

"Girl, I'm just calling to give you the details of my date," Jordan sang.

"Well by the mood you're in, it's safe to assume that your date was a success," Diamond smiled as she backed out of her parking spot and pulled into traffic.

"Hell yes! Taj is one hell of a man, D. He's tall, dark, handsome, intelligent and a boss!" she squealed. "I know I went out with guys before that were making a lil bit of money illegally, but Taj got legal money. I'm not sure what he does, but I know he's an entrepreneur of some sort and so is his friend that I tried to hook you up with. We got another date set up for in a couple of weeks, and I'm not taking no for answer this time," Jordan stated sternly.

"Aww Jay," she whined. "I already told you how I felt about this. If I wanted to go on a date, I probably coulda set one up the other day."

"Hold the hell up. What happen the other day? Some nigga tried to holla at you?"

"More like pay for me and my co-worker's lunch. He had his waiter bring us a note on a napkin offering to pay for our lunch. I wrote no and gave the napkin back to the waiter. When we got up to leave, I walked over to his table, told him I'll pay for his lunch, slid him three hundred dollars and walked off," she shrugged as she took the ramp to the expressway.

"Wait a minute. You gave that nigga three hundred for lunch and then left? What the fuck did you do that for?"

"I did that to show him that I don't need no man to do shit for me. He looked like the type of nigga that was used to getting any woman he laid his eyes on. So for me to drop a couple of C notes on the table and then leave, I'm sure that shit bruised his ego a lil bit," Diamond chuckled.

"Damn D. You cold blooded," Jay laughed. "What did he look like? Was he cute? Did he look like he had money?"

DIAMOND & BOSS

"Judging from the Armani suit, Rolex and his iced out pinky ring he was rocking, the nigga definitely had some money. He kinda looked like Rick Ross a lil bit but not as fat, and yes. He was very handsome."

"He sounds like he might be a boss himself. Don't be surprised if that nigga decides to hunt ya ass down."

"Please. That nigga ain't gonna come looking for me. He probably got a bitch for all thirty days of the month." Diamond dismissed her friend's comment. "What you getting into tonight, Jay?"

"I'll probably slide through and come chill with you and lil bro."

"That's cool. Make sure you bring some liquor. I already got food."

"Cool. See y'all tonight."

"Aight."

Ending the call, Diamond drove the rest of the way to her job, parking in the underground garage. When she made it to the fourteenth floor of the Municipal Service Building, she got comfortable at her desk and got right to work. Diamond needed to make sure things were in order for a test that was being given for the Firefighter and Correctional Officer position the following day. The candidates that met the requirements were emailed with the time and location where the test was being held. About fifty people or more showed up to take these exams, but only a few actually passed and got hired. The benefits that came with working for the city was worth the hassle of trying to get hired.

Keeping herself busy for most of the morning, by the time Diamond looked at the clock, it was after one in the afternoon. Removing her phone from her purse, she checked it to see if she had any messages or missed phone calls. When Diamond saw that Justin had texted her, she opened it.

Justin: Aye sis. I'm hanging out with my homie Rico

after school. We're gonna be working at his cousin's clothing store in Mt. Airy every weekend starting today and I'll be spending the night with him, too. The clothing store is in the Cedarbrook Plaza where the Walmart is. The owner, Rico's cousin, wants to meet with you to discuss this with you. You can meet me there when you get off work. The owner's name is Q but everyone call's him Boss. See youlater

Diamond reread the text before tossing it back in her purse. The fact that her brother was about to start working on the weekends made her wonder what his reason was for wanting a job. Most fifteen-year-old boys were looking to make money the fast way. They were either trying to hit a lick or sell drugs to get money. Diamond couldn't help but smile when she thought about how responsible her brother was trying to be. Since she had to meet her brother after work, Diamond decided to work through lunch, so she could leave early.

When quitting time approached, Diamond said her goodbyes before grabbing her things and heading out the door. Riding the crowded elevator to the main floor, she made her way to the underground garage, hopped in her car, brought it to life and pulled out of the lot into traffic. Drake's Scorpio album filled her car as she maneuvered through the streets of Philly. Pulling into the Cedarbrook Plaza thirty minutes later, Diamond parked in the nearest spot. She removed her phone from her purse before hopping out the car. She caught the eyes of a few men that were passing by, but she didn't pay them any attention. As she walked inside the store, she spotted her brother and another boy checking out the sneakers.

"Yo, bro," Diamond called out, getting his attention.

"Aye D. I wasn't expecting you to be here this early," Justin greeted her with open arms.

"I skipped lunch so I could be here early," she embraced him. "Is this your friend, Rico?"

"Yup. Rico, this is my sister, Diamond. D, this is my homie Rico."

"Nice to meet you Miss Diamond," Riko smiled.

"Same here, and drop the Miss. You just made me feel old," she laughed. "So Justin, what's the deal with this job? You never told me you were thinking about working."

"That's because this was something that I wanted to do on my own. I know you've been picking up extra hours so you can have more money to support us and that doesn't sit right with me. So I figured if I got a job, I could help out and take some of that stress off you," he answered with a straight face.

"Wow Justin. I...I don't know what to say," Diamond's eyes began to well up with tears.

"You don't need to say anything, sis. I love you and appreciate how you stepped up and took me in when mom left. You coulda put me in the system, or sent me to live with family, but you didn't. The least I can do is help you carry the load."

Diamond tightly hugged her brother as she fought back her tears. Hearing that her brother appreciated her for taking him in and him wanting to help out, melted her heart. She thought her brother's head was filled with school, girls and sex, but knowing that he was also willing to lighten the load she was carrying, showed her that he was trying to be a man.

"I love you lil bro and appreciate you wanting to do this, but I don't want you to use your money on bills. I want you to spend your money on you. That means you're responsible for your haircuts, your bus fare, clothes, sneakers and your weekend activities. If you need help paying for something, I'll help you, but you need to show me that you can be responsible with ya money and not squander it. If you need me to show you how to manage your money, I will. So, do we have a deal," she extended her hand.

"Deal," Justin shook her hand with a smile. "Thank sis."

"No problem. Now where is this Q?"

"Right here," a deep baritone voice responded from behind her.

Turning around, Diamond's eyes bucked at the sight in front of her. When she realized that it was the man from the restaurant, her heart began to beat out of her chest.

"Well, well, well. We meet again," he smiled at her.

"I guess we do," Diamond responded dryly. "I'm Diamond, Justin's sister."

"Nice to meet you. I'm Boss but you can call me Quentin. If you'll step into my office, we can get this meeting started."

"Lead the way."

Quentin looked her up and down before walking to the back of the store with Diamond following him from behind. She couldn't believe that the man her brother was about to start working for was the man from the restaurant. As they entered his office, Diamond got a whiff of his cologne and found herself stepping closer to him to smell it again. Getting lost in the scent, she took a moment to get herself together, putting her game face on before taking a seat in one of the chairs in front of his desk. If her brother was going to work for Quentin, Diamond needed to know everything about this man and his establishments.

CHAPTER 6

"First things first," Boss cleared his throat. "How are you doing today?"

"I'm fine," she folded her hands in her lap. "Not to be rude, Quentin, but I would like to discuss the business at hand, if you don't mind," Diamond sternly stated.

Diamond's tone of voice instantly irritated Quentin and turned him on at the same time. He wasn't used to women being short with him, or giving him attitude and the women that did, he dismissed them bitches and kept it pushing. But receiving this rude treatment from Diamond had him feeling some type of way, and he couldn't understand why.

"No problem," he got into business mode. "I'm sure Justin informed you of why you're here."

"Yes, he did. Justin told me that he was going to be working in your store on the weekends starting today."

"That is correct. His starting position will be a sales associate, but for this first month, Justin will only be training. The first Saturday in March, he will be on his own. If he does well in training and proves that he can step out on his own before then, I will have him working on his own sooner.

Since this is technically his first job, his starting pay rate will be thirteen dollars an hour, but once he completes his training, his pay will increase to fourteen-fifty an hour, and he will get annual raises if I feel as though he deserves it when it comes time for his annual work evaluation," Boss explained, looking Diamond in her eyes.

"So far so good," Diamond's eyes remained trained on his. "Justin also mentioned something about spending the night over your house every weekend. What is that about?"

"My younger cousin, Riko, has a situation going on at home and I convinced my aunt into letting me take him under my wing and be a mentor to him. Him spending the weekend with me was part of the deal. Riko asked if Justin could work for me and hang with us on the weekends, and I told him it wasn't a problem. Now, Justin spending the weekend at my crib is not mandatory. I can either drop him off at his house, you can pick him up, or he can catch the bus if you don't feel comfortable with him spending the weekend with us."

The room fell silent for a moment as they continued to stare at each other. Boss was confident that Diamond was on board with Justin working for him, but she was very hesitant about him spending the weekend with him.

"If you have any questions, feel free to ask," Boss leaned back in his chair.

"Is this your only business or do you have others?" Diamond inquired.

"No, this is not my only business. I have six establishments throughout Philly. This particular one has been opened for four years now. I've been an entrepreneur for a decade and all of my businesses are very successful," he answered with confidence.

"Are any of your establishments being used for any illegal activity?"

"Excuse me?" Boss became defensive.

"It's just a question," she held her hands up.

He bit the inside of his jaw before responding.

"No. All of my businesses are free from all illegal activity," Quentin tried to hide his irritation. "May I ask the reason behind the question?"

"I asked because if my brother is going to be your employee and mentee, I need to know that you're walking the straight and narrow. Too many of these businesses are being used to clean drug money and everything else, and I don't want Justin to be associated with any of that. So, if you can give me your word that you can be a positive influence in my brother's life and teach him how to be a man, I will allow Justin to work for you and hang out with y'all on the weekend," Diamond pleaded.

Hearing Diamond's explanation caused Quentin to instantly ease up. He could tell that she truly cared about her brother and the activities he was involved in. He also knew that her brother was all the family she had for real, and the last thing Quentin wanted to do was put Justin or his cousin in harm's way.

"You have my word, Diamond," he answered sincerely.

"Cool," she nodded her head. "Do I need to sign any documents, or will you be paying Justin under the table?"

"There are a couple of documents that need your signature," he opened the folder that was on his desk. "This form is for him to get his work permit and this is a consent form for him to be employed at the store," Quentin pushed the papers in front of her.

He watched Diamond as she read the documents before signing them. Although he was professional, Quentin couldn't help but to take in all of her features. Her beautiful brown eyes, cute button nose and full lips made it hard for him to look away from her. Her feistiness should have turned him off, but it only attracted him to her even more.

"It's not polite to stare," Diamond removed a pen from the holder, signing the forms.

"I apologize. It's just that I never expected you to be this feisty," he chuckled.

"I apologize if I came across rude. I'm just a lil over protective of my brother. I had a tight hold on Justin since I got custody of him, and now that he's about to start working and spending the weekends away from me, I don't know how to feel about that," she replied solemnly.

"I understand that, but you can't keep him under lock and key forever. Growing up is a part of life."

"I know," Diamond sighed.

"So, do you care to explain why you paid for my lunch," Boss removed the $300 dollars from his pocket, dropping it on the desk.

"That was my way of letting you know that I'm an independent woman, and whatever you *think* you can do for me, I can do for myself," she answered boldly.

"Damn. It's like that?"

"Straight like that."

"Well, I got your message loud and clear, but your money is no good here. I'm a man in every aspect of the word and I don't need a woman to support me, but the gesture was appreciated. That was the first time a woman ever offered to pay for anything when it came to me," he licked his lips.

"That doesn't surprise me," she chuckled. "Is there anything else you need from me?"

"No. That's it. It was nice meeting you, Diamond," he extended his hand.

"I know it was," she responded cockily. "If anything happens to my brother, just know that I'm licensed to carry, I go to the gun range often and my aim is on point. So, you better take care of my lil brother. You hear me?" Diamond warned, standing to her feet and shaking his hand.

"Yes ma'am," he smirked at her.

Diamond removed one of his business cards from the holder and the money from his desk then tucked them in the pocket of her blazer.

"Enjoy the rest of your day, Quentin," she headed out the office leaving the door open.

Quentin watched her seductively as Diamond switched out of his office. The way her jeans hugged her round ass caused his dick to jump in his pants. Her body and the warning she gave him had Quentin about to lose his damn mind. Whenever a woman was in his presence, they were always shy, sweet, flirtatious, sexy and seductive. They damn near did anything to get his attention and it took little to nothing to get them into bed; but Diamond was the complete opposite. Her personality was bold, feisty and down right mean. She had no problem letting him know that she didn't need him for a damn thing and didn't care how he felt about it. She was definitely a challenge, and he debated with himself on if he wanted to accept it. Why would he struggle to get pussy that probably wasn't worth the hassle? But what if it was? Instead of weighing the pros and cons at that moment, Quentin pushed his thoughts of Diamond to the back of his mind.

A few minutes later, he called Riko and Justin into his office and helped them fill out their job applications, W-2 and I-9 forms, and the form for their work permit. When he saw that he was going to need their birth certificates and social security cards, he had them call their parents and ask for them. After they filled out the forms, the trio grabbed their things leaving the store. Rico and Justin couldn't start training until they obtained their work permits so, Quentin decided to call it a day. Popping the locks to his truck, they hopped inside and he brought it to life. Cautiously pulling out of the spot, he drove through the lot then drove into traffic. Lil Wayne's Carter Four album played as he maneuvered through the streets heading to his home in Bucks County Pennsylvania, which was located on the outskirts of Philly.

As he got closer to his house, Quentin glanced over and saw Riko and Justin gazing out the window admiring the neighborhood they were driving through. He could tell by the looks on their faces that they were shocked by the sight before them. All of the houses he drove past had manicured lawns and bushes. They also had tall trees surrounding them, and some of the houses had gate entrances. Not to mention, the neighborhood was very clean. In Philly, trash decorated the hood streets and depending on the area, not many of the houses had trees, grass, front or back yards. Trips to the suburbs were taken for shopping purposes, which didn't happen too often. Quentin knew that the boys were out of their comfort zone, but part of his plan was to teach them that there was more to life than just hood shit.

Forty-five minutes later, he entered the cul-de-sac, made a few twists and turns, then pulled into the driveway of his home.

"Damn, Boss," Riko hopped out the car with his duffle bag hanging from his shoulder. "I don't think you ever brought me out here."

"This is my new crib. I only had it for a few months. I'm renting out my other crib and call me Quentin. Only my employees call me Boss," he secured the car with the remote.

"Ain't we your employees, too?" Justin asked with his bags in hand.

"Yeah, but y'all are also family, but just know that when y'all start working for me, I'm gonna hold y'all to a higher standard than the rest of my employees. Just keep that in mind."

Unlocking the front door, they entered the house and Quentin gave them a tour of it. The four-bedroom, three-bathroom home was an open floor plan with high ceilings. The kitchen had granite counter tops, forty-two cabinets with brick backsplash and top of the line appliances. A brick, wood-burning fire place was located in the great room along with built-in window seating and skylights. The fully finished walk out basement was equipped with a full bar, media room, and recreation area which opened onto the paver patio and luxurious pool area, with gorgeous landscaping; it was perfect for outdoor pool parties.

Ending the tour in the basement, Riko and Justin didn't hesitate to hop on the PS4. The 75" smart TV was bolted to the wall and was connected to a surround sound system. The black leather sofa had recliner chairs on each side with a matching glass coffee table in front of it.

"Yo Q, ya house is everything man. Thanks for inviting me," Justin grinned.

"No problem, but don't thank me. Thank ya sister. Without her approval, you wouldn't be sitting here right now," he chuckled.

"Diamond seems tough, cuz. How'd you get her to say yes?" Riko glanced up at him.

"I gave her my word that I wouldn't let nothing happen to J, and I always keep my word."

"I hope so, because D gonna kill ya ass if you don't," Justin laughed.

"Don't I know it," he mumbled. "Aye what y'all want to eat? I know y'all hungry."

"Pizza and wings," they responded in unison.

"Aight. Don't mess up my house because if y'all do, ya asses won't be back."

Jogging up the stairs, Quentin made his way to the kitchen taking a seat at the counter. His phone began to ring in his pocket and he knew it was Bashir calling. He hadn't spoken to him all week to see how well he could handle things on his own, and by what he saw on the cameras, he seemed to have things under control. Removing the phone from his pocket, he answered the call.

"Wassup Banks? How are things going with the club?"

"Everything is going just fine man. The furniture, glasses and décor came today. I have an interior decorator coming on Monday and the stereo equipment is arriving on Wednesday. We just have to get started with the hiring process, place the order for the alcohol and start spreading the word about the grand opening," Bashir responded confidently.

"Cool. Cool. Call Kamaya so she can start advertising for the club and I'll be there early Monday morning to talk to the interior decorator."

"Can you call Kamaya? You know me and shawty don't get along like that."

"Me and Maya on the outs for two weeks for the that shit that happened at the party, but I know how y'all feel about each other, so yeah. I'll call her."

"Thanks. What you got planned for the weekend?"

"I'm chilling with my lil cuz and his homie this weekend. Well every weekend, unless something comes up. They're gonna be working in the clothing store on the weekends and I'm gonna be mentoring them."

"That's wassup. These lil niggas need a real one to look up to. Might as well be you," Bashir chuckled.

"I guess," he chuckled as well. "Aight let me order this food man, and I'll catch up with you on Monday."

"Aight."

Ending the call, Quentin called Pizza Hut and placed the order before shooting a text to Kamaya letting her know to start advertising that the club was hiring. She responded okay, then he cleared the screen and checked his email. He saw that he had one from Diamond. She sent him the items he needed for Justin to get his work permit and Quentin replied to the message with Thank You. Thinking of the conversation they had earlier, his dick became semi erect as he thought about her body. Everything in him warned him to stay away from her, but it was something about her that made Quentin want to get to know her.

The fact that she had been taking care of her brother for the past five years told him that she was all about family, but he had a feeling that the abandonment of her mother made her the strong, independent woman that she was. After spending minutes contemplating on how he wanted to handle Diamond, Quentin decided to accept the challenge and try to get to know her. Hoping for the best, he had to mentally prepare himself for whatever his feisty target had to throw at him.

CHAPTER 7

After ending the call with Quentin, Bashir walked to the kitchen area of the club and made sure the stove was operating properly, and it was. He checked the fridge to see what kind of condition it was in as well as the light fixtures. After making sure everything was functioning properly, Bashir decided that he wanted the kitchen remodeled. Since everything else in the club was brand new, the kitchen should be as well. Shutting the lights off, he headed back upstairs to the office, taking a seat behind the desk. He waited a few seconds for the iMac to load then searched the web for businesses that remodeled kitchens. Bashir grabbed his notepad and pen then jotted down the name and phone numbers of the businesses. He saw that most of them were closing soon, so he decided to give them a call first thing in the morning. Shutting the computer off, Bashir stood up to leave when there was a knock on the door.

"Come in," he called.

When he saw that it was Kamaya, Bashir frowned his face up.

"Boss ain't here," he spat in annoyance.

"I can see that. He just sent me a text telling me to start advertising for the club and I needed some details. Where is he?" Kamaya walked inside the office.

"I don't know, but I guess I can tell you what you need to know."

"You can't tell me shit because you don't call the shots, and if you think you can tell me something, Boss has to confirm everything," she stated boldly.

"Being as though I'm the one running this shit, I can guarantee that Boss will back up whatever decision I make," Bashir cockily smirked.

"Nigga you know damn well Boss ain't letting you run this club. You might be his business partner, and he taught the tricks of the trade, but you don't have what it takes to successfully run a business. So, miss me with that bullshit."

"Look bitch, I know you were one of the many people that told Boss not to make me his business partner and you had it out for me since I stepped on the scene, but you need to face the fact that I ain't going no fucking where. So, you better learn how to play nice because if you keep disrespecting me, ya ass gonna come the fuck up missing," he stepped from around the desk.

"Ooooo, I'm shaking in my stilettoes," Kamaya laughed. "Don't you ever in your life fucking threaten me," she stepped closer to him getting in his face. "Boss might be letting you run the show with this business, but *Boss* is the one that *finalizes all* the decisions. So whatever details you tell me now, I'm gonna run them by the *real* HNIC before I put anything the fuck in motion."

Standing inches away each other, Bashir was ready to put a bullet through Kamaya's skull. He hated her ass with a passion, and he wasn't sure how much more he could take of her dissing and disrespecting him. Bashir was clueless as to what he did to Kamaya to make her treat him the way she did, but he was going to put an end to that shit one way or another.

"Okay Kamaya," he ran his hand over his face, "Boss will be here on Monday and since he has ya ass on punishment for two weeks, I'll let him know that you will be joining us, so you can get the specific details you need to do your job," he smirked.

"Fuck you Banks," she turned on her heels to leave.

"You probably want to. Maybe that's why you're so hostile towards me," he joked before the door slammed. "That bitch gonna make me kill her one of these days."

Shutting off the lights in the office, Bashir locked the door before turning the lights off in the building and locking it down. Hearing a car horn, he smiled when he saw it was his fiancée, Morgan, pulling up in his white 2018 Lincoln Navigator. He jogged over to the car, kissed his girl then hopped behind the wheel. Bashir looked in the backseat as he buckled his seatbelt and saw their one-year old daughter, Maria, sleeping in her car seat.

"Y'all must've had a full day," he shifted the car from park to drive. "Baby girl knocked out back there," he chuckled.

"Yes, we did," Morgan giggled, "After we picked my mom up, went out to breakfast, hit up Willow Grove Mall, took Maria to Chuck E. Cheese and chilled with my mom until it was time for us to leave. She said she sends her love."

"I know you're lying, but okay."

"My mother loves you, Bashir. I don't know why that's hard for you to believe," she shook her head.

"I know the difference between fake love and real love. Your mother doesn't like me. She tolerates me because you love me and we have a child together. There's a big difference," Bashir boldly stated.

"Anyway, how was your day?"

"It was great. The club is really coming along. I can't wait until it opens. That shit is going to be lit," he smiled.

"That's wassup, bae. I knew you would do great on your own if you had the opportunity to do so."

"Yeah. I'm grateful for the opportunity, too. Boss didn't have to put me in the front line with this. I'm gonna have to do something grand to show my gratitude."

"If you prove to him that he didn't make a mistake with his decision, I'm sure that will be gratitude enough," Morgan remarked. "You know Boss don't really go for gifts and shit."

"I guess you're right."

The car fell silent for a moment before Morgan spoke.

"Baby are you happy with your life?"

"What? That's a random ass question," Bashir glanced over at her.

"I know it is, but it's something that's been on my mind. I know you've adjusted to making legal money, but I can't help but wonder if this is really what you want to do," she spoke softly.

"I'm not gonna lie and say that the transition from the streets to the legit life has been easy. I mean, taking orders from another nigga and following another man's lead is something that I don't think I will ever get used to, but it was change that needed to be made and meeting Boss gave me a fresh start. I'm glad that I can rest easy at night knowing my family is safe and I don't have to look over my shoulder. So, to answer your question, yes. I'm very happy with my life," he smiled at her.

As he drove to his suburban home in Franklin Lakes, New Jersey, Bashir thought about his old life and why he decided to leave the streets. Throughout his childhood, he was known as a goody two shoes and mama's boy. He didn't go anywhere or did anything without his mom and did anything to make her proud. His siblings and cousins used to tease him because he was also known as the snitch of the family. When he went to visit his cousins, they always distanced themselves from him and left him by himself. As he got older, Bashir grew tired of being a mama's boy, goody two shoes and snitch, and that's when his life took a drastic turn.

At the age of fifteen, Bashir became fascinated with the neighborhood dope boys. He admired how the girls reacted to them, how much money the had and the cars they drove. Whenever he would go outside, he would watch them from his steps and wondered what it would be like to get money like them. Tired of wondering, Bashir went to his best friend of the same age and asked him to put him on. After his friend gave him the run down of the streets, the products and prices, his friend gave him dub bags of weed to sell. As his friend observed Bashir from a near by car, he was posted on the corner serving work. Within two hours, he'd made three hundred dollars. When the weed was all gone, he went to give the money to his friend and he told him to keep it. That was the day that him and friend became partners. It was also the day that changed his life forever.

Although he was a full-blown hustler, he didn't let the streets interfere with school or his grades. He was the valedictorian of his high school's graduating class, and had scholarship offers from a few universities but once he was out of high school, he dedicated his life to the streets. By the time he was twenty, Bashir had made a name for him and earned the respect of everybody in his neighborhood as well as the people in his family. Whenever someone would tease him or diss him, he whopped their ass until they were damn near dead. Whenever he became angry, it was hard to calm Bashir down.

His temper got him into a lot of unnecessary beefs over the years. His best friend warned him repeatedly about his temper, but he never listened and when his friend came up with the idea to expand their business from weed to cocaine, he cut Bashir out of the deal and brought in someone new. Feeling hurt and betrayed, he tried to his best not to take his friend's decision personal, but he couldn't. Bashir felt as though he should've still been apart of the deal, regardless of his temper. They were friends, and they started that shit together, but since it was so easy for his friend to cut him off, it would be easy for Bashir to kill him, which he did, before he robbed him.

Spending the next three years of his life hitting licks and robbing the major drug dealers in different cities, Bashir had accumulated more money than he could even count and the best part about it was that he didn't have to split the profits with anyone. He rode solo and that's how he liked it because he didn't have to worry about being betrayed or cast out. Hitting licks was all he cared about, and getting money was all he cared about. He fucked plenty of bitches over the years, but he never kept them around because they would only slow him down. But when he met Morgan, everything changed. He fell in love with her the moment he saw her ordering food at a Wawa's in New Jersey. He tried to have a balance between his old life and his new one, but when the last robbery ended with him almost dying, Morgan begged him to call it quits, and he did.

A year and a half into the relationship, Bashir had tried working a regular nine to five, but that life wasn't for him. The thought of starting a business entered his mind and he began to research what he needed to start one. He saw an article on Quentin Marks and his decade long success as an entrepreneur amongst his searching. Impressed by what he read, Bashir found his contact information and called Quentin's office. After telling him the nature of his call, Quentin invited him to come to his office for a meeting.

Their meeting lasted for two hours. After explaining his life and current to situation Quentin, he told Bashir to come back the next day for his training. He spent six months learning the ins and out of each business before he was assigned to manage the barbershop. His first couple of months there, someone shot up the barbershop and the employees felt like Bashir was the target because that was the first time the shop was ever shot up.

The shop had been broken into a couple of times over the years, but nobody attacked them during business hours. When the customers heard about the shooting, some of them stopped coming and they lost a few dedicated barbers because Quentin decided to keep Bashir around. Instead of waiting to be told what to do, he stepped up and fixed whatever damage was done to the shop. He personally sat down with the barbers who decided to leave and ensured their safety and gave them five-hundred dollars to sign back on with them. They decided to give Bashir another chance. Since then, the barbershop has been running smoothly, the employees respected him, and no one has been harmed or hurt in any way.

Bashir played a part in every business they had when he hit the one-year mark. From organizing meetings, to terminations, he knew how to professionally handle business without losing his cool.

In the beginning, he wasn't feeling all the training he had to do and when people blamed him for the shooting, Bashir was ready to say fuck it and walk away, but he was glad that Morgan talked him into staying because if he would've left, that would've showed Quentin how weak he was and that he couldn't handle the ups and downs of entrepreneurship. Bashir believed that his hard work, determination and loyalty earned him a shot to run the club and he was going to take advantage of it.

Pulling into the driveway of their four bedroom, three-bathroom Colonial home, he killed the engine to his truck then hopped out.

"Baby, can you grab the bags out the trunk please," Morgan called, unstrapping Maria from the car seat.

Popping the truck, Bashir shook his head at the many shopping bags that took up all of the trunk space. He grabbed the bags with both hands, carrying them upstairs to their room and placing them in their walk-in closet. Closing the closet door, he kicked off his shoes before sitting on the bed. He heard Morgan clear her throat and when he saw her standing in the doorway naked, Bashir quickly removed his Polo t-shirt, wife beater and True Religion Jeans. Walking over to him, Bashir watched her as she removed his boxers, swiftly inserting his dick in her mouth.

"Fuck bae," he groaned watching her deep throat his nine-inch shaft.

Grabbing a hand full of her curly Brazilian hair, he tossed his head back as her speed increased. Feeling himself about to cum, Bashir pulled her up to her feet and she climbed on top of him. Morgan sat on him and began bouncing up and down on his dick, using her feet.

"Shhiittt," she moaned placing her hands on his chest.

Bashir bit his lip, watching the sex faces she made and the way her 40DD titties were bouncing. Grabbing them, he played with her nipples using his thumbs and gently squeezed her breast.

"Oooo, Daddy! I'm about to cum!" Morgan groaned.

Placing his hands on her waist, Bashir began roughly deep stroking her pussy, causing her juices to squirt all over his dick and lower stomach. He continued his pounding until he filled her insides with his seed. Morgan collapsed on top of him as they both tried to calm their breathing. He wrapped his arms around her moist body and prepared to get comfortable, but it was short lived when they heard their daughter crying in the other room. They exchanged a quick kiss before they dragged themselves out of bed. Bashir slapped Morgan's bubble butt as she slipped her robe on and left the room. Entering the master bathroom, he stepped into the stand-in shower, turning the water on. Bashir listened to Morgan as she played with their daughter in their room and smiled. Life was better than he could ever imagine. With him practically running his own business and having a beautiful fiancée and daughter, Bashir felt like he'd finally accomplished something positive in his life. He was only twenty-six and living a life that most people dreamed of, but his was a reality and he was going to do anything to keep it that way.

CHAPTER 8

Since her meeting with Quentin, Diamond was having a hard time adjusting to her brother being gone. She was used to them spending the weekends together, or him hanging out on the weekends with his friends, then returning home. Not him being gone from Friday until Monday afternoon. It took everything in her not to blow his phone that weekend, but Jordan convinced her to leave him alone. When Justin returned home on Monday, Diamond hugged him tightly and didn't want to let him go. She missed her brother, and she thought that he'd missed her, too, but when Justin revealed to Diamond how much fun he had training at the store and he spent the weekend playing video games, learning how to play pool and having guy talk, she realized that Justin didn't miss her as much as she thought he would, but Diamond was happy that he enjoyed himself.

As the weeks passed, Diamond continued to bust her ass at work and school. Although Justin was working and making his own money, she still picked up extra hours and the money that she used to spend on him, Diamond deposited that money into her savings account. Even though he was only in his sophomore year, she figured she'd start saving for his prom. It felt weird to her that she no longer had to take care of Justin's expenses. For the past five years, everything Diamond did was to provide a better life for her and her brother, but now that he was taking care of himself, she was starting to feel like Justin didn't need her anymore.

After taking exams all week, Diamond was glad when Friday rolled around. She was beyond exhausted from all of the studying and all the work she'd done that day. It had her feeling like she was ready to fall over. The last thirty minutes of her shift, Diamond fought to keep her eyes open, but when she walked out the front doors of the MSB, she came alive a little bit. As she headed towards her car, her phone began to ring. Knowing it was Jordan, she answered as she climbed in her car.

"Hey Jordan."

"Hey girl," she greeted excitedly, "Are you ready for tonight?"

"I'm really not, but I'm still going," she sighed pulling out of the underground garage.

"You damn right you are. It's been years since you've been on a date and it's time for you to get back into the game," Jordan sternly stated. "Did you get your outfit and shoes?"

"Yup, they came the other day, but I don't know if I'm going to wear that dress. It's too sexy, J."

"There's no such thing. You're going to look great and we're going to have a good time tonight. Taj is sending a limo to pick us up tonight. So be at my house by 7:30pm."

"I'm about to go home, grab my stuff and just go to your house now. I need a nap and if I fall asleep at my crib, I might not wake up," Diamond laughed.

"Yeah. Just take ya ass to my house and I'll wake you up when I get there."

"Aight. See ya later."

Hearing Drake's 'Nice for What' playing on the radio, Diamond turned up the volume and sung along to the lyrics as she headed home. Pulling into the parking lot minutes later, she noticed a car parked in front of her building as she parked. Diamond saw the Uber sticker in the front windshield as she passed to enter the building and disregarded her suspicions. Unlocking the door to her apartment, she saw Justin coming out of his room with his duffle bag in hand.

"Hey, lil bro. What you doing here?" She stood in the doorway.

"I forgot my clothes because I was running late this morning for school," Justin answered.

"You coulda asked me to bring your clothes to the job. It wouldn't have been a problem, J."

"I know sis, but I figured you might be tired from work and school and I didn't want you to go out ya way," he replied sincerely. "My Uber is waiting for me. I love you. See you on Monday," he quickly kissed her cheek closing the door behind him.

Diamond shook her head at her brother as she headed to her room. Opening her closet, she grabbed her new dress that was still in the package along with her new shoes that were still in the box. She grabbed her shawl from the top shelf, causing a few things to fall. Diamond debated on whether or not she wanted to pick up the small mess. Sucking her teeth, she placed her clothes on the floor next to her as she began cleaning up. Her heart sank to her feet when Diamond saw an old picture of her and Damien. It was the day she graduated from Temple University and the day he proposed to her. In the picture, she was holding her degree up in her right hand and showing off her two-carat princess cut diamond engagement ring as he hugged her from behind, with Justin standing next to her. Unable to hold back her tears, Diamond began to cry as she continued to stare at the picture. A part of her wanted to call Jordan and cancel her date because she wasn't ready to move forward and let go of Damien. They had spent four years together, and he was there for her when Diamond's mother disappeared. Damien took Justin to school in the morning, so she wouldn't be late for class. He even helped her brother with his homework, so she could do her assignments and study for her exams. If it wasn't for Damien, Diamond probably would've had to drop out of school and get a full-time job just to support them. The role he played in her life during that time was major and she loved him for how he stepped up and helped her. Although she was thinking about canceling the date, Diamond didn't. Jordan was right, it was time for her to move on.

Wiping her tears, she collected the rest of the things off the floor, placed them back in her closet, grabbed her clothes and headed out the door, locking it behind her. Diamond power walked to her car to get out of the cold. She brought the car to life then sped out of the lot, heading towards Jordan's house that was twenty minutes away. Parking in front of her house, Diamond noticed a black 2015 Chevy Impala with tinted windows parked across the street with the engine still running. Grabbing all of her things, she jogged up the steps onto the porch, using her key to get in. Diamond dropped her things on the expresso color leather sofa then peaked out the window to see if the car was still there, and it was. Jordan had been living in that house for a year and a half, and Diamond never saw a car like that or any car with tinted windows parked up on her block before. She knew that any car that had tinted windows was up to something shady, and it made her a bit uncomfortable. She stayed in the window for a few minutes before taking her things upstairs to the guest bedroom, where she took her nap.

"Diamond…. Diamoonndd…wake up?" she heard a soft

voice calling her name and shaking her. "Come on girl. It's time for us to get ready for our date."

"Already? I feel like I just laid down," she mumbled as she sat up.

"It's a little after 6:30. You probably got here around five so an hour and half of sleep should be enough rest to get you through this date," Jordan chuckled, "Now, let's go."

Slowly getting out of bed, Diamond went into the closet removing the huge Victoria's Secret bag that was full of new underwear she had left there for times like these. She pulled out the leopard print seamless panties and strapless bra set, then placed it on the bed. Taking her dress from Fashion Nova out of the package, Diamond laid it on the bed admiring it for a second before heading to the bathroom. She twisted up her curly Brazilian weave, placed the shower cap on her head, then disrobed, stepped in the shower and turned the water on. As she grabbed her rag and lathered it with Dove soap, Diamond couldn't help her nervousness. The thought of her going out with a man she'd never seen before had her on edge.

Once she was finished in the bathroom, Diamond went back into the bedroom and began getting dressed.

"Oooo, I can't wait for you to meet Taj," Jordan shouted down the hall, "That nigga so fine, D. I get goosebumps every time I think about him."

"I can't wait to meet him, either. Any nigga that got you gone like this must have a dick made of gold," Diamond teased as she slipped into her underwear.

"Shut up ho," Jordan laughed.

"But seriously, I am looking forward to meeting him, but I'm a little on edge about meeting his friend," she expressed. "What if he's ugly, Jay? What if we don't have anything in common?" Diamond fastened her bra.

"First of all, Taj told me that his brother will be joining us and if I'm telling you that my nigga is sexy, that nigga gotta be sexy, too, or at least cute. Secondly, stop tripping. I've seen you hold conversations with boring people before. You can handle this," she coached her friend. "But even if homeboy is ugly, I still want you to try and look past that and make the most of the night. Aight?"

"Aight, but if the nigga is ugly, I'm cussing you and Taj out at the end of the date and putting ya ass on the block list for a month," she warned.

"Deal."

Diamond applied lotion to her body before slipping into her leopard print spaghetti strap bodycon dress, then slid her feet into her gold, blinged out Michael Kors peep toe platform pumps. She put on her gold necklace, hoops and Michael Kors watch before letting her curly weave cascade around her face. After applying her mascara and lipstick, the doorbell sounded throughout the house. Admiring herself in the mirror, Diamond hardly recognized herself, but she looked damn good, to say the least.

"Damn, girl. Ya ass is looking hella juicy in that dress, boo. You gonna make that nigga wanna take you home," Jordan boosted.

"I know he's gonna want to, but he can only look, not touch," Diamond winked.

"I think you'll be singing a different tune when the night is over," she smirked. "Grab ya purse and let's go."

Taking a quick selfie with her phone, Diamond tossed it in her gold clutch purse along with her lipstick, wallet and keys before draping her silk shawl around her, turning the lights off and leaving the room. When she reached the bottom of the stairs, the duo left out the house making their way down the steps. They were greeted by the limo driver as he held the door open for them. Once they were inside, he closed the door and took his place behind the wheel, then pulled off.

"This limo is nice as fuck. I haven't been inside of a limo since our senior prom," Jordan beamed.

"Yeah but our limo was basic. It wasn't as fancy as this," she pointed out. "They got champagne on ice and a phone back here."

"That's what I'm talking about. A bitch can get used to this," Jordan grabbed the champagne and filled the glasses, passing one to her bestie.

"You always had a thing for the lavish life," Diamond stated sarcastically.

"Quiet as kept, so have you, because if you didn't, you wouldn't be walking around wearing designer labels of any sort."

"I guess you're right about that."

They sipped their drinks in silence.

"I know we've always took pride in spoiling ourselves with the finer things in life, but what's wrong with a man spoiling us with those things, too?"

"Ain't nothing wrong with a man showering a woman with gifts. I just feel like a woman should be able to buy those things for herself as well. Do you know how many thots and gold diggers that are walking around rocking top notch designer fashions and purses but can't maintain that lifestyle if they nigga stopped footing the bill for them? You gotta be able to provide that shit for yourself, because if a nigga decides to leave you for the next bitch, how are you gonna be able to maintain that lifestyle?" Diamond preached.

"I hear what you're saying and you're right," her bestie agreed. "I know a few bitches that can't even go out to eat at an expensive restaurant without their nigga footing the bill for it. I like having my own shit, so I don't have to depend on a nigga."

The girls chatted for the rest of the ride to the restaurant. They reminisced about old times and the double dates they used to go on when they were teenagers. If somebody would've told Diamond that she and Jordan were going to be friends for a decade or more, she wouldn't have believed them. They started out as rivals and competitors in middle. The competed for damn near everything. Whether it was for President of the student body or the captain of the cheerleading team, they always went head to head. They were equally tied for wins. People would tell them that they needed to be friends because they had so much in common, but they never listened until they found out that they liked the same boy and he was playing them against each other. Diamond and Jordan jumped the boy and had been best friends ever since. As they got older, they were known as Thelma and Louise because you never saw one without the other, and if you did, it was only because they had separate classes. Even though they were as thick as thieves, the duo had their share of fights and problems, but no matter what, they were always there when they needed each other, and their bond only became stronger over the years.

When the women arrived at the restaurant, the limo drive opened the door for them helping them out of the car. They thanked him before heading in the restaurant, which crowded. Instead of waiting in the short line, the duo headed to the front where the hostess booth was, gave her their names and the hostess didn't hesitate to have someone escort them to their party. Diamond and Jordan walked arm and arm as they followed the waiter to the back of the restaurant and to a private area. Diamond's heart began to beat out of her chest as they got closer to the table. Spotting the two men sitting at the table, one of them had their backs to them, but when the men saw them coming, they stood to their feet and Diamond's mouth hit the floor when she saw who her date was for the evening.

* * *

"It seems like we just keep running into each other, huh Miss Diamond?" Quentin smirked.

"Oh. So y'all know each other already?" the light skin chick pointed between them.

"This is Quentin. The guy Justin is working for and his mentor," Diamond folded her arms over her chest, "So if you're here, who's supervising my brother?"

"They're at home by themselves. I have cameras in my crib, so I know everything that they're doing. You can relax," he chuckled.

"So, this is the woman that you were telling me about?" the tall, dark and handsome man smiled.

"Yes it is. Taj, this is Diamond. Diamond, this is my younger brother Taj," Quentin introduced them.

"It's nice to meet you," Taj extended his hand to her.

"Same here," she lightly shook his hand, "I've heard a lot about you."

"And Q, this is my lady Jordan."

"Nice to meet you, Jordan. It's a pleasure to meet the woman that stole my brother's cold heart," Quentin teased making the women giggle.

"Cut it out man," Taj nudged him. "Shall we sit?"

"If it's alright with Diamond, I would like for us to dine alone," he stared at her, waiting for her to answer.

Quentin watched her look to her friend for her answer and Jordan nodded her head yes.

"Okay," Diamond shrugged.

"Cool. Y'all enjoy y'all evening," Jordan sang, as her and Taj walked a few tables down from them.

"May I help you with ya wrap?"

"Sure."

He stood behind her and slowly removed the shawl from Diamond's shoulders. Quentin's eyes damn near popped out their sockets when he saw how her dress hugged her curves.

"Damn Diamond," he whispered staring at her ass.

"What did you say?" she turned around to face him.

"I uh...I said you look very beautiful this evening," Quentin nervously smiled.

"Mmm hmm," she smirked as she sat down, "If I woulda known that I was having dinner with you, I probably wouldn't have shown up."

"Well, I'm glad you didn't know because I was actually looking forward to seeing you again," he licked his lips seductively.

"Is that right?" she grabbed a menu off the table looking it over.

"Yes it is. I don't come across too many that play me to the left and now that I have, I would like to get to know you better," he responded honestly.

Placing her menu on the table, she stared into his eyes for a moment before speaking.

"Look Quentin, if your only interest in me is to wine, dine and fuck me, we need to change this conversation right now. I don't have time for anyone that's going to play with my emotions, make me fall and as soon as I give him some pussy, he up and disappears because I played him to the left," she boldly commented.

"Damn. Someone must've have done a number on you, huh?"

"Not at all. I hear the stories woman tell and I will not be one of the women that that has happened to."

The waiter came to take their food and drink order. Quentin let her first then gave his own. After reciting the order back to them, he scurried to Taj and Jordan's table to take their order.

"I know a lot of niggas be out here playing games with women, but I'm not that type. If all I wanted was sex, I would let you know that, and I wouldn't have brought you no dinner to tell you so."

They both laughed.

"I didn't say it to be funny. I'm just stating the facts. I feel like if you just tell a female what you want, things will a go a lot easier for these niggas," he added.

"So that works for you?"

"It has so far," Quentin shrugged. "But that's not my intentions with you. I would like to be the man you call when you need someone to talk to and the man you want to hang out with. What I'm saying is that I would like for us to be friends and get to know each other. Maybe we might even turn into something more," Quentin took her hands in his, "So, what do you say?"

They stared at each other for a moment as he waited for Diamond to answer. By the way her eyes kept shifting from his to the table, he could tell that she was struggling to make up her mind. If Diamond was against them getting to know each other, she would've had no problem telling him no but since she was taking her time to decide, Quentin was confident that she might give him a chance.

"I tell you what, if this date goes well, then yes. We can be friends and get to know each other," Diamond shifted her eyes back to his, giving him a small smile.

"I can deal with that," he licked his lips seductively.

The waiter returned with their appetizers and drinks, then placed them on the table in front of them. Quentin admired how Diamond said a silent prayer before taking a forkful of her giant crab cakes. The face she made when she tasted it made him smile.

"This is the best crab cake I've ever tasted. My compliments to the chef," she took another forkful and gave the same reaction.

"I might have to give him a raise if he keeps getting reactions like that," Quentin stated nonchalantly eating one of his stuffed mushrooms.

"Wait a minute. You mean to tell me that this is your restaurant, Quentin?" she asked in shock.

"Why yes, it is," he grinned.

"Well I'll be damned," she chuckled, "I thought you were just trying to impress me when you said you had multiple businesses throughout Philly. Now I see why they call you Boss?"

"You thought I was spitting game, huh?"

"Hell yeah," she laughed, "No offense, but niggas out here will lie about a lot things if they think it would put them in good standings with a female."

"You ain't never lied about that shit," Quentin chuckled in agreement, "But that's not me."

"I see that now," she seductively smirked at him.

Feeling her eyes on him, Quentin glanced up at her and Diamond quickly looked away causing him to smile. He could tell that she was fighting to keep her guard up but he was hoping that he would earn some cool points by the end of the night. As the evening went on, Quentin was surprised at how comfortable he was conversing with Diamond. He discussed things about himself that he never told another female. He told her about his eventful childhood, his parents and the unbreakable bond between him and Taj. Quentin shared stories about their ratchet teen years to the ump teen ass whoopings they received for the dumb shit they did. He got a kick out of seeing Diamond laugh and smile at the stories he told and she shared some of her own. As he listened to her talk about her fatherless childhood, besides the fact that her mother was desperate to have a man in her life, he was impressed of how Diamond knew at a young age what traits to pick up from her mother. She also talked about her friendship with Jordan, but when he learned about her ex and the role he played in her life as well as Justin's, his heart broke for her.

"That's why it's been kinda hard for me to date anyone after all these years. I felt like since he was the man I was going to marry, I had to continue to be loyal to him. Even from beyond the grave," Diamond took a sip from her second glass of green apple Sangria.

"I'm sorry for your loss, Diamond," he sincerely commented, "I can't imagine how hard that must've been for you. What made you decide to move on after all these years?"

"I finally decided to take Jordan's advice and move on with my life. I'm only twenty-five and I shut myself off from men for three years. I don't wanna be old and alone. I would like to share my life with someone that will love me the way that I'm gonna love them."

"I'm glad that you decided to take a chance with this date. Maybe I'm the one you're looking for," he smirked.

"Or maybe you're not," she smirked back and they laughed.

"Would you care for some dessert?" The waiter asked, clearing off their table.

"I would like a slice of strawberry cheesecake to go, please," Diamond ordered, taking a sip of her drink.

"No problem ma'am. Anything for you Boss?"

"Naw I'm good T. Thank you."

"Quentin, I hate to admit this but, I really enjoyed dining with you this evening," Diamond softly spoke.

"I'm happy to hear that. So, does that mean we're friends now?"

"I guess so," she shrugged.

"Cool. Do you mind if I ask for your number?"

"Give me your phone."

Obeying her command, Quentin handed over his phone and watched her as she typed her number in. As she passed the phone back to him, it began ringing in her hand and when it saw that it was Kamaya calling, he instantly became angry. Declining the call, he placed his phone in his pocket and sighed.

"Are you okay?"

"Yeah. I'm fine. I'm just regretting a decision I made a while ago."

"And what was that?"

"Crossing the line with someone I do business with," Quentin confessed.

"Oh. I see," Diamond nodded, "We all make mistakes. It's how you go about fixing it that matters," she encouraged.

"Here's your cheesecake ma'am," T handed her the bag with a smile.

"Thank you and this is for you," she handed him a twenty-dollar bill.

"Thank you," he smiled, before strolling away.

"You didn't have to do that."

"I know, but since you're paying for dinner, I figured I'd take care of the tip."

"I hate to interrupt y'all. I just wanted to ask Diamond was she ready to go," Jordan approached the table.

"Yeah. I'm ready."

"Okay," she smiled at them before walking back to her table.

"Diamond, I hope that phone call I received didn't make you feel uncomfortable," Quentin helped her out of the booth.

"No it didn't, but I'm sure I don't have to tell you how to handle your affairs," she put her shawl on.

DIAMOND & BOSS

"What's that supposed to mean?"

"It means that if you have intentions on being with someone, you shouldn't make that person feel like they have to compete for your attention. I know you have numerous females in your life, but if you plan on being with one of them, you know what you gotta do with the rest of them," Diamond sternly stated.

"Have a good evening gentlemen and Taj, it was nice to meet you again," she smiled.

"Same hear. Jay, let me know y'all made it home safely," Taj kissed Jordan's lips.

"I will. Nice meeting you Quentin."

"Nice meeting you."

Quentin locked eyes with Diamond for a moment before the women headed down the hall to leave. Rubbing his beard, he took a seat at his table with his brother sitting across from him.

"So Q, how did the date go? Do you have a new friend or what?" Taj inquired.

"I do have a new friend, but I think that's all we might be?" Quentin took a sipped of his double shot of henny.

"Why you say that?"

"She basically just told me that if I had intentions on being with her that I would I have to let go of all the females I fuck with. I don't even know if the pussy good and she's telling me what to do," he shook his head.

"Calm down, bro," Taj chuckled, "I'm sure she wasn't telling you what to do, but letting you know what you're gonna have to do if you want to be with her and from what you told me about her, you shoulda known that Diamond wasn't gonna be cool with you fucking with other females," he added.

"We're just friends right now, so I don't have to do shit at the moment. I'm just gonna take my time and get to know her first. I already feel like I'm doing too much to get her already," Quentin complained, "You know I told her about my childhood, our parents and the shit we used to get into when we were kids?"

"Get the fuck outta here," he shouted.

"Yeah man. I feel like the dude on that movie 'Think Like A Man' when he was dating Megan Good and she had them talking about their childhoods and their feelings and shit," Quentin ranted.

"Wow! I think you might actually like shawty," Taj teased.

"No, I don't," he denied, "Diamond is cool and we did have a good time tonight, but I'm keeping her feisty, demanding ass in the friend zone. I'm Boss and don't trip over no bitch," Quentin cockily stated.

"Keep telling yaself that," Taj laughed, "but on another note, how's everything going with the club? I know the grand opening is in a few weeks, right?"

"Yeah and I'm hype. My partner is really on his game with this shit. I didn't really have to correct anything. He got that shit set up to perfection. I got good vibes about this shit," he took another sip of his drink.

"That's wassup, and you said your partner is running it?"

"Yeah. Banks has been shadowing me for two years now. He got in contact with me and told me how he wanted to start a business of his own. So, I showed him the ins and outs of all the businesses I had, and since he proved to me that he can handle things on his own, I decided to let Banks run the club."

"I'm gonna have to meet this dude. Anyone that has earned the trust of my brother is someone I definitely need to know," Taj downed the rest of his Corona.

"I'm assuming you'll be at the grand opening?"

"Wouldn't miss it for the world, bro."

The duo spent the next hour discussing their business

plans, collaboration plans and the women in their lives. Quentin was shocked to learn that Taj was considering making Jordan his girl. After his girlfriend of six years confessed that the baby she was carrying wasn't his, he swore that he would never get into another relationship again but learning that his little brother was considering it made Quentin think twice about settling down.

When they decided to call it a night, the brothers exchanged a quick hug as valet brought their cars around. Hopping inside his truck, Quentin shifted the car to drive, heading towards the expressway. As he nodded his head to Rick Ross's 'God Forgives, I Don't' album, the ringing of his phone interrupted his groove. Seeing that it was Kamaya calling again, he answered.

"What, Maya?"

"Hey, did I wake you?" she asked softly.

"Nah, I'm on my way home. Wassup?"

"On ya way home from where?"

"If you must know, I had a date."

"A date?" her sweet tone was replaced with base and attitude.

"That's what I said."

"Okay…um…I was calling to let you know that I'm going to be shutting down the hair salon for a week a so for remodeling purposes. Some of the hair dryers are messing up, the tiles on the floor are coming unloose and the bathroom needs to be redone," she pulled herself together.

"Okay. Did you call our company for an estimate?"

"Yeah. They said it was going to run us between ten and twenty thousand depending on how bad the damage is."

"Damn," he blurted out. "Let me make a few calls and I'll get back to you."

"Aight."

Letting out a sigh of frustration, Quentin pulled into the

driveway of his home, killed the engine and hopped out of the truck. He went inside of the house and expected to hear loud music playing and a bunch of noise, but he didn't. It was quiet throughout the house. A little too quiet. He checked the basement first in search of the boys, but they weren't down there. He headed upstairs and heard voices coming out of Riko's room. Peeking his head inside, Quentin saw that his lil cousin was lying in his bed, boo loving. Quietly closing the door, he walked to the next room peeking his head inside Justin's room where he was sitting at the desk with his phone propped up against the wall, talking to a girl on FaceTime that was helping him with an assignment. Before closing the door, Quentin over heard Justin asking the girl out on a date and when she told him that her father wouldn't let her go out without a chaperone, an idea popped into his head of him being their chaperone but before he did that, Quentin had to teach them the basics of how to properly court a girl.

Quentin headed to the master bedroom where he sat on the bench at the end of his bed. He slipped off his Stacy Adams dress shoes before removing his suit jacket, tie, shirt and pants. Carrying his clothes over to the walk-in closet, Quentin hung the suit in a long suit bag with the rest of the suits he'd worn for the week. He grabbed a pair of gray Nike sweat pants and slipped them on. Sliding the door shut, Quentin snatched his phone off the bench then got comfortable in his California king size bed. He sent a text to his brother letting him know to hit him up in the morning to discuss business then turned on his 60-inch smart tv and flipped through the channels and stopped on ESPN.

As he caught up on the latest basketball scores, thoughts of Diamond entered his mind. Replaying their date, Quentin couldn't help the smile that appeared, but instantly removed it from his face. No matter how hard he tried to front, he couldn't deny the affect that Diamond had on him. Although he accomplished his goal, which was to get her to let her guard down, Quentin didn't realize that he'd let his guard down as well. He didn't lie when he said he wanted to get to know Diamond, but that didn't mean he was ready to cut all of his chicks off and be a one-woman man. As much as he enjoyed their date, Quentin wasn't ready to pursue Diamond fully. He was going to continue to do him and deal with her when he was ready to.

CHAPTER 9

Tossing back her second shot of peach Cîroc, Kamaya sat at the bar, pissed off. She couldn't believe that Boss had went out on a date. Since her two-week punishment ended, she had been on her best behavior, and kept her attitude at bay. Whenever she had to meet with Boss and Banks, Kamaya kept her rude comments to herself and did whatever was required of her, with a smile. She even held her composure when other women made passes at him in her presence when ever they were out in public together. Although they hadn't spent any evenings together, Kamaya was satisfied with the breakfast, brunch and lunch dates they had together and the quickies they got in whenever they could. With all the attention Boss was giving her, she was convinced that he was starting to view her as his one and only, but now, Kamaya wasn't so sure that he did. After learning about his date, she couldn't help but wonder who Boss was spending his nights with since he wasn't spending them with her.

Hearing her phone vibrate on the counter, Kamaya checked to see who was calling and instantly declined it.

Ordering three more shots and some food, her phone started ringing again and she did the same thing. She picked her phone up placing it face down on the counter.

"So you just gonna keep declining my calls like I'm one of these clown ass nigga you be talking to," a husky voice spoke from behind her.

"Yup because that's what you are," she stated snidely.

"What the fuck you just say?" The man expressed with anger.

"Because you are, Garrick," Maya turned to face him. "You pop the fuck up outta nowhere talking about you miss me and shit. You wine, dine and fuck me for nearly a month then turn around and ask me to set up a business meeting with my fucking partner? That's some clown ass shit if you ask me," she added in disgust.

"So me asking you to put in a good word for me with one of the biggest bosses in Philly is a clown move?"

"It's the way you went about it. You didn't have to kick game to me and make me feel like ya ass really missed me. I woulda respected you more if you woulda came to me straight and just told me what you wanted," the bartender placed her drinks in front of her. "How the fuck did you find me anyway?"

"This was our favorite place to hang out when were dating. So, I figured I'd pop up to see if you were here," he answered. "I guess a nigga was on ya mind?" he smirked.

"Not at all," she shot him down.

"Damn Maya. That was cold."

"Look, Garrick, I'm not setting up a meeting for you with Boss, so can you please leave me alone? If you want to meet with him, set that shit up ya'self, but I'm warning you now. He doesn't associate with your kind," Maya tossed one of her shots back.

"What the fuck you mean he don't associate with my

kind? He got something against niggas that've been to prison?"

"Not at all. He doesn't fuck with drug dealers or niggas affiliated with the streets. Boss always got his money the legit way, and he doesn't want to do business with anyone who was a part of that life."

"That's why I need you to put in a good word for me, baby," he leaned over and began kissing on her neck. "Come on, Maya. I'm trying to get this business started and if I have Boss as a partner, I know this shit will be successful," Garrick pleaded.

"Now why would I fuck up the empire Boss and I built together, to take a chance on you? You told me that you left the streets alone, but by the way ya phone is blowing up, I beg to differ. It might be bitches calling you, but I got a feeling that it's fiends calling for drugs," she pushed him away from her. "You thought fucking me and whispering sweet nothings in my ear was going to make me decide in ya favor but ya plan failed. I'm not the same bitch I was seven years ago, Garrick. I wised up and started dealing with men that were about something and stopped dealing with street niggas. Yeah, you played me, but I won't let you do it a second time," Maya harshly stated.

"I see you started making a lil bit of money and ya ass done got uppity," Garrick smacked, "Aight, Maya. You don't have to help me. I'm gonna get my business up and running with or without ya help," he snatched one of her drinks and downed it, "I'll be seeing you again soon," he got up and left.

Unfazed by Garrick's remarks, Kamaya finished her last drink before her food came. Finishing her food minutes later, she paid her tab then staggered out of the bar getting into her car and starting the engine. She took a few moments to get herself together before pulling out of the spot and heading home.

Kamaya cursed herself for falling for his lies and deception like she did when they were together. He used sex as a way to get her to do whatever he wanted, which almost lead to Kamaya spending the rest of her life in jail. Garrick fucked her so good that she agreed to taking a trip for him, but he never told her what she was dropping off or picking up. Before she made it to her destination, Kamaya was pulled over by the cops and arrested. When she learned about what was in the trunk of the car, she broke down and cried but instead of snitching, she kept her mouth shut. Due to her mother pulling a few strings, Kamaya was able to walk out of there a free woman. When she tried to get in contact with Garrick, his phone had been disconnected and his apartment was abandoned. Feeling like a fool, she vowed to never get mixed up with niggas like him again, but she broke that vow when he popped up at the salon a couple of weeks back.

When Kamaya made it to her condo, she carried herself to her room, flopping down on the bed. Happy with the decision she made to not do business with Garrick, she forgave herself for falling for his lies, then drifted off to sleep.

CHAPTER 10

"Daammmnnn. That shit feels good," Quentin hissed as he received head from one of his out of town chicks.

He watched her as she made his eight-and-a-half-inch shaft disappear in her mouth. The way she licked his dick like a lollipop made his eyes roll into the back of his head as he gripped a handful of her short, natural hair.

"Not uh, nigga. I told you about my hair," she quickly stopped sucking to check him.

"My bad," he chuckled.

Quickly fixing her curls, the dark skin beauty continued sucking his dick like her life depended on it.

"Fuucckk. I'm about to cum," he groaned.

Seconds later, Quentin released his load into her mouth and she swallowed every drop. Taking a minute to get himself together, he finally stood to his feet, tucked his shirt in and fixed his pants while his soul snatcher fixed herself up as well.

"Damn, girl. I see you haven't lost ya touch," he smirked, sitting behind his desk.

"No I haven't," she grinned, "I figured while I was in town helping with this Gala, I would stop by and see one of my top donators and to give one last memory of me."

"Let me guess, you're tired of the flings and ready for a real relationship."

"I'm getting married in two months and wanted to get you out of my system. This had been and annual thing for us over the past five years and I wanted to end it on a high note. I've been faithful to my fiancé ever since I met him, but I couldn't fight the urge of having you inside me and blessing you with some head," she smiled seductively.

"Yeah our sex sessions do be something epic. Ya man is getting one hell of a lady for his wife."

"Thanks Boss," she blushed, "Now you will be in attendance at the Gala this weekend, right?"

"Yes I will be there with my plus one."

"Are you bringing *her*?"

"If you're referring to Kamaya, yes. She is my partner."

"Okay. I already talked to Taj and he said he'll be in attendance too with his plus one. Here are y'all tickets and there is no theme this year," she grabbed her purse, "Well, I gotta go. It was nice seeing you again and thank you for a wonderful time."

Quentin came around his desk to hug her. Kissing her cheek, he broke their embrace before Taj and Kamaya came into his office. He examined how Kamaya and his sex partner grilled each other as the dark-skinned chick passed her.

"See y'all at the Gala on Sunday," she sang as she left.

"See ya," Taj waved before closing the door.

"Please tell me we're not going to that damn Gala again," Kamaya sat in one of the office chairs in front of his desk." I can't stand being around those snobs," she rolled her eyes.

"Funny. I thought that was your type of crowd. You

mingle with them so well," Taj sarcastically remarked, causing Quentin to chuckle.

Peeping the way she was glaring at him, he stopped his laughing and placed his focus on the computer monitor.

"Well, since I have to attend this event, I need a breathtaking gown," She rose to her feet. "Taj be a dear and fill your brother in about the salon," Kamaya left out the office.

"I don't know how you deal with shawty, man. She's the fuck annoying. The whole time I was checking out the building, she asked me a million and one questions about how long I've been in construction, where did I go to school to get my license, why don't I reside in Philly, why don't you want to settle down, why are you a ho and blah blah blah. I told her I was there to do a job. Not socialize," Taj got up from his seat and headed over to the liquor cabinet.

"Damn. She called me a ho?" He chuckled," I guess the real question is why does she keeping fucking my ho ass?"

"Nah. The real question is why did you fuck her in the first place?" Taj poured him and his brother a drink. "You already know you're not supposed to cross the line with your employees or business partners," he placed a glass in front of Quentin and sipped his before sitting back down.

"I know that man, but after she helped me win the building for the breakfast shop, I went to give her a kiss on the cheek and she kissed my lips. Next think you know, I'm ripping off her clothes and fucking her on my desk," Quentin sighed. "I know I shoulda cut that shit short, but the pussy is too good man," he shook his head. "Besides her being in her feelings about me fucking other bitches, Maya is smart, sexy and a damn beast in this industry. She's part of the reason why my businesses are excelling the way they are. I think I'm in too deep for us to just cut off the sexual aspect of our relationship to return things to the way they were."

"I can understand why you feel that way, but the only

reason you slept with her was because she made the first move. If Maya wouldn't have shown no signs of interest, you wouldn't have given her the time of day and you know it. She became an easy mark for you. You don't never go for a woman that challenge's you or that's gonna make you respect her. I think that's why you're avoiding Diamond."

Quentin gave his younger brother the stare of death as he let Taj's word, register. Unsure of how to handle his brother's truthful comment, he decided to avoid it.

"You don't know what you're talking about Taj," he dismissed his brother's comment. "Anyway, you bringing Jordan to the Gala?"

"You know I am. I thought you were gonna bring Diamond instead of Kamaya. I don't know how well the women are gonna get along with each other because if Maya gets outta line, ain't no telling how Jordan is gonna react," Taj held his hands up.

"Well hopefully the women can play nice for the evening and keep the cattiness to a minimum."

As they sipped their drinks, Quentin listened as his brother told him the work that needed to be done at the salon, and how much it was going to cost. When Taj suggested that the entire inside of the shop be remodeled, he instantly began to stress, but when his brother told him that he could have his men get started on the building ASAP and he was only going to charge his brother ten grand for everything, Quentin was grateful. Quentin thanked Taj for helping him with his building.

Quentin called his brother around to the other side of the desk so he could see how the club was coming along.

"I feel some type of way that you didn't ask me to do the construction and the remodeling on the building man," Taj mean mugged his brother.

"My bad bro. From now on, you are my main contractor for all of my businesses."

"That's one way to fix this," Taj's eyes remained on the screen. "Who's that?" he pointed to the screen in the corner.

"That's my homie, Banks. He's running the club."

"Zoom in on him."

Confused, Quentin did as he was told. Once the screen was enlarged, he watched how his brother's demeanor changed as Taj continued to stare at the monitor.

"You said his name is Banks?"

"Yeah."

"What's his real name?

"Bashir Phillips. Why? Wassup?"

"Nothing," he answered angrily. "Look, I'ma holla at you. I gotta check into something. Me and my workers will be at the salon at seven. If I need you, I'll call you," Taj stood to his feet to leave.

Standing to his feet, Quentin gave his brother a quick hug before watching Taj storm out of his office. Confused, he sat back down in his office chair and stared at Banks on the monitor. An uneasy feeling came over Quentin as he pondered as to why Taj reacted the way he did when he got a good look at Banks. Although the sirens were going off in his head, he decided to act as if nothing was wrong and monitor all activity with Taj and Banks closely.

CHAPTER 11

"You don't know how pissed I was when Taj told me that Quentin was going to the gala with his business partner," Jordan scoffed, "And the fact that that nigga hasn't called you all week got me ready to come at his neck. Who the fuck does he think he is, D?" she added from the passenger seat of Diamonds' car.

Diamond laughed at her friend as she ranted on about Quentin's disrespect. Although she was upset that he hadn't contacted her in a week, she wasn't letting it bother her. Despite what he told her on their date, a part of Diamond knew that his ass was all talk. She knew that Quentin was used to women throwing the pussy at him, and since she wasn't making things easy for him, she didn't expect him to come around anytime soon. Diamond was looking forward to getting to know Quentin, but the last thing she was going to do was chase him or wait for his ass to come around.

"Calm down Jay," she placed her hand on her friend's shoulder. "Do you see me tripping or hear me complaining? I'm good, girl. I ain't tripping on Q," Diamond put her middle finger up as if he could see it.

"Well if you cool, I'm gonna chill but all you gotta do is say the word and I'll get at his ass," she stated.

"I know you will," Diamond laughed. "Besides, just because Quentin didn't invite me to the Gala doesn't mean I'm not gonna be there," she smirked stopping at a red light.

"Don't tell me ya crazy ass is thinking about crashing the Gala? You know we don't do ratchet shit like that now," Jay shot her a disapproving look.

"Bitch, no. I ain't that pressed to go, but one of my co-workers asked me to be his date for the Gala," she replied pulling off when the light turned green. "He doesn't seem like the type that knows a lot of important people but like they say, never judge a book by the cover."

"Aawww shit now! My bitch is gonna be in the building after all! I feel better about going now," Jordan cheered, "Quentin gonna be sick when he sees you there with another nigga."

"You think so?"

"Hell yeah! Taj told me that he's fighting his feelings for you because you got standards and ya feisty ass ain't for the dumb shit. He knows that in order for him to be with you, that ass gonna have to straighten up and fly right, but he's definitely feeling you sis, and when he sees you with ol' boy, that's gonna fuck Quentin's head up something serious," she stated.

"This evening is going to be more fun than I thought," Diamond grinned devilishly.

Diamond parked across the street from the hair salon fifteen minutes later. Grabbing her True Religion mini backpack, Diamond locked the car door and paid the meter for up to two hours before the duo headed inside the semi crowded salon. As Diamond and Jordan waited to get their hair shampooed, her phone began to ring and she knew it was her brother by the tone. Seeing that Justin was facetiming her, Diamond connected the call.

"Hey baby bro. What's good with you?"

"I'm good. I'm at work about to go out on the floor. Where you at?"

"At the salon with Jordan. I need my hair done for my date tonight."

"Date? You go out on dates now?"

"Yes, I do, Justin. Is that a problem?"

"And when did this start?" He questioned."

"My first date was last week if you must know, and tonight will be my second, and no its not with the same dude."

"I don't know how I feel about you dating," he twisted his face up," Especially since I ain't there to meet any of the dudes."

"Check you out being all over-protective and what not," she chuckled," I know you didn't call to be in my business. So, what do you want?"

"I was calling to see if you were free tonight, so you could chaperone my date with Kailyn," answered sadly.

"Kailyn? That's the girl that was walking by the Boys and Girls Club that day, right?"

"Yeah," Justin blushed. "Her mom finally agreed to let her go to the movies with me, but she can only go if we're chaperoned, but you're going out tonight."

"Why didn't you tell me this sooner, Justin?"

"I didn't think you had anything to do. You never go out on the weekends," he shrugged.

"I don't have anything planned for next weekend. So, I'll take ya'll then. Aight?"

"That's cool with me. Thanks sis. You're the best. I love you."

"Love you too lil bro. Have a good day at work," she smiled.

"I will."

Tucking her phone in her back pocket, Diamond shook her at her brother.

"Damn. Lil bro is growing up for real, huh?" Jordan looked up from her phone. "Justin just asked you to chaperone his first date. How do you feel about?"

"Like I'm in over my head, and that I'm getting old," she shook her head before picking up one of the magazines.

"Awww. Why?" Jay gave her bestie her attention.

"Because when we were coming up, we didn't have chaperoned dates with boys. We went on group dates. Us, three or four other girls from school and the matching number of boys."

"I remember that," she laughed. "And we would act a damn fool when we went out sometimes. We had to stop going to the mall with the boys because they were always stealing."

The girls laughed in unison.

"Right but we had fun to say the least," Diamond calmed her laughter, "I just feel like this is a job for my mom. I didn't know all this responsibility would come with taking in my brother. I thought all I would have to do was take care of him until he turned eighteen then he was free to do what he wanted. I didn't think about the in between stuff like him having sex, dating, him holding down a job and all the rest of life lessons that I basically had to learn on my own," she huffed.

"Aye, I watched you struggle with taking care of your brother. So, you *know* I know what you had to go through to get to where you are, and I must say you are doing a hell of a job raising your brother," Jordan sincerely spoke.

"Thanks Jay," she briefly hugged her friend," but I can't

take all the credit anymore. Since Justin has been hanging with Q, he's changed. Jus is taking care of his responsibilities as far as buying his bus fare and his hair cuts, but yesterday, he gave me his half of the money for his cell phone bill and that wasn't part of our deal. On top of that, his grades are still on point. I didn't think Justin was going to be able to manage everything, but he's proving me wrong," Diamond bragged.

"Damn. So, Quentin is actually doing a good job with the boys, huh?"

"I hate to admit it, but he really is."

"I still don't like his ass for the way he's treating you, but I gotta give him props for what he's doing for the boys. Fatherless boys need some type of positive male role model in their life."

"You're right about that," Diamond agreed.

After a fifteen minute wait, the duo were called over to the sinks to get their hair washed. Diamond removed her headphones from her backpack, attached them to her phone and listened to her tunes. She played games on her phone to kill the time as well as made small talk with her stylist. About an hour and a half later, the ladies' Brazilian body wave weaves was slayed, and their eyelashes were on fleek. Once they paid and tipped their stylist and shampoo girls, Diamond put some more quarters in the meter before they headed down the street to the nail salon.

After allowing their nails and toes to dry, the women paid for their services then made there way to Diamond's car and headed back to her apartment. When the duo made it back to Diamond's apartment, she began making lunch for them while Jordan made Long Island Ice Teas for them to sip on. As she sautéed the chicken breast she was cooking, her phone rung.

"Guess who this is calling me, Jay?"

"Don't tell me that's Quentin?" she jumped up from the kitchen table.

"It sure is," Diamond chuckled, "I guess Justin must've mentioned my date tonight."

"Are you gonna answer?"

"Nope," she placed the phone on the counter," Let's see if he calls back and if he does, I'll answer," Diamond winked.

"You are something else, girl," Jay laughed, "Quentin done found the right one to fuck with ,because you are gonna put his ass through the ringer."

"You damn right, I am."

The phone stopped ringing and Diamond continued cooking her food. Ten minutes later, her phone rang, and again, it was Quentin.

"Put it on speaker so I can hear," Jordan laughed.

Obeying her friends command, she put the call on speaker phone before answering.

"Hello?"

"Yo, wassup with you?" his deep voice boomed through the phone.

"Excuse me?" Diamond instantly caught an attitude.

"I know you saw me calling you. Why you ain't answer?"

"First of all, you need to take some of that bass out ya voice when you're talking to me. Second, when you call my phone, you greet me first before you start coming at me like you're crazy; and third, I didn't answer my phone because I didn't want to. This is my phone and I can pick and choose who I want to talk to," she spoke sternly.

Silence filled the room for a moment.

"You know what," Quentin sighed, "You're right. I shouldn't have come at you like that and I apologize. Can we start over?"

Quickly looking over at Jordan whose mouth was gapped

open, Diamond was surprised by his response, but continued the conversation.

"Yes. We can start over."

"Hello Diamond. How are you doing today?"

"I'm doing fine, Quentin," she finished cooking the chicken, "How are you?"

"I'm aight," he replied in a calm, sexy tone. "I just wanted to touch bases with you to let you know a nigga ain't forget about you. I've just been busy."

"It's cool, and I understand," Diamond rolled her eyes.

"I know this ain't my place to ask but Jus told me that you're stepping out tonight. Is that true?"

Hesitant, Diamond didn't know why she felt as though she should lie, but she didn't.

"Yes. It's true."

The phone fell silent but this time, it was awkward.

"Hello?" she spoke.

"Yeah. I'm still here. Uh… have a good time on your date, aight? I'll…I'll hit you up later."

The call ended, and Diamond stood at the counter stuck in place, clueless as to what had just happened.

"Oh my God," Jordan broke the silence, "That nigga feels some type of way that you're going out tonight. He's gonna flip his shit when he sees you at that Gala tonight."

Still stuck, Diamond remain quiet.

"D, are you okay?"

"I was about to lie to him about my date, Jay," she answered in a trance, "Why would I want to do that. Quentin doesn't mean anything to me."

"Or maybe you like him more than you're letting on."

Taking a moment to get herself together, Diamond put the chicken in the salad she prepared for them and made their plates before placing them on the table. They chatted about the evening and what they expected it to be like since neither of them had attended an event like that before. As the time winded down, so did Diamond's confidence. She was having second thoughts about attending the Gala because she didn't want Quentin to see her out with another man. She didn't know what changed her mind about the evening, but Diamond still decided to go through with it. She felt like if he saw her out with another man that it would make him step up and stop being scared of a challenging woman, and if it didn't, Diamond was cool with them staying at the level that they were.

* * *

Dressed to the nines, Quentin and Kamaya stepped inside the Pennsylvania Convention Center where the Gala was being held. The duo was all smiles as they shook hands and exchanged hugs with the familiar faces in the crowd, as they made their way to their table. The chandeliers that hung from above sparkled throughout the building. Waiters and waitresses were scattered throughout with trays of champagne, making sure everyone had a drink. The tables were decorated with white and gold linen table clothes, with a vase of white roses for the centerpieces.

"This place looks beautiful," Kamaya gasped, "They seem to make this event better every year. Don't you agree?"

Lost in thought, Quentin didn't respond.

"Quentin?" she nudged him.

"Huh?"

"What's with you?" Kamaya stopped in her tracks. "You've been distant since you picked me up. Are you okay?"

"Yeah. I'm fine," he lied, giving her a small smile.

They continued walking and when they spotted Taj and Jordan, Quentin felt Kamaya tense up.

"Why didn't you tell me that Taj was bringing one of his

groupies to the Gala?" she asked with disgust lacing her voice.

"Jordan ain't no groupie. That's his lady and you will respect her. Do you hear me?" Quentin turned her towards him, so he could look into her eyes.

"Yes," she frowned.

Making their way over to the table, Taj and Jordan stood to greet them.

"You looking good bro," Quentin and Taj exchanged a quick hug.

"Yeah. You know I can clean up nice when I want to," Taj bragged.

"And Jordan, you're looking beautiful as ever this evening," he kissed her cheek.

"Thanks Quentin," Jordan smiled before her eyes landed on Kamaya.

"Kamaya this is Jordan, Taj's lady. Jordan, this is Kamaya. My business partner."

"Charmed," Maya greeted dryly.

"Like wise," Jordan answered just as dry.

"How about we have a seat," Taj suggested.

The men held the chairs out for the ladies before they sat down next to each other.

"There are a lot of heavy hitters here tonight. This might be a good time to scan the room and see what's the talk around the industry," Quentin whispered to his brother.

"That doesn't sound like a bad idea," he replied as he scanned the room with his eyes, "Aye, will ya homie Banks be joining us this evening?"

"Nah. I didn't tell him about this. He gotta crawl before he can walk," Quentin harshly stated. "Why do you ask?"

"It was a just a question," Taj answered with his hands up, implying that it was innocent.

Quentin and Taj stared at each other for a moment and

he could tell that his brother was keeping something from him, but instead of speaking on it, Quentin nodded his head to let him know that everything was cool. The waiter brought a tray of champagne to their table and every took a sip from their glass. As Quentin observed his surroundings, thoughts of Diamond entered his mind. Since their phone call earlier, all he thought about was her being out with another nigga. He tried to convince himself that he didn't give a fuck about what she did or who she went out with, but Quentin was just lying to himself. The thought of Diamond being in the presence of another man bothered the fuck out of him, but he didn't understand why.

"Yo Q," Taj tapped his arm forcefully.

"Wassup?"

"You're not gonna believe who's here," his brother's eyes were locked on whoever was behind him.

"Who?"

"Turn around man, but whatever you do, don't flip out," Taj warned.

Turning around, Quentin almost dropped his glass when he saw Diamond with her date. He couldn't believe how beautiful she looked in her wine-colored halter high-low dress, honey blonde and light brown curls, with her silver, ankle-strap peep toe pumps. Quentin couldn't take his eyes off her and he couldn't control the anger that was starting to consume him. Seeing that Diamond was headed in their direction, Quentin was the first one to his feet to greet them. Noticing the couple, Kamaya stood up as well as Taj and Jordan.

"Good evening all," Diamond strolled over with a smile on her face.

"Oh my God, Diamond. You are stunning honey," Jordan snapped her fingers admiring Diamond's dress, before hugging her.

"Thanks bestie," she cheesed. "And you are wearing the hell outta that dress," Diamond complimented her.

"Diamond, I almost didn't recognize you girl," Taj hugged her.

"You look very handsome tonight Taj, and so do you Quentin," Diamond broke their embrace.

"Thank you," Taj responded.

Quentin remained silent.

"Everybody, this is Kyle. Kyle this is my best friend Jordan, her man Taj and his brother Quentin," she introduced everyone.

Everyone gave different greetings, except Quentin and Kamaya.

"I'm Kamaya, Quentin's business partner," she introduced herself.

"That's nice," Diamond politely dismissed her, causing Jordan to laugh out loud. "Well, y'all enjoy the rest of the evening," she smiled before walking off.

Quentin stared Diamond down as they walked off with her arm looped in his. He couldn't believe that she was bold enough to show up to the same event he was attending on the arm of another man. A part of him felt disrespected, but Quentin knew he couldn't blame anybody but himself.

"Quentin, who the fuck was that bitch?" Kamaya stepped in front of him blocking his view of Diamond.

"Who the fuck you calling a bitch, ho!" Jordan tried to step closer to Kamaya, but Taj grabbed her, dragging her to the dance floor.

"First of all, don't disrespect her like that and secondly, Diamond is just a friend," Quentin sat down at the table, taking his glass of champagne to the head.

"A friend?" She sat down next to him, pulling her chair closer to his. "What type of friend? A friend with benefits? A friend that gives you head? What?"

"If you must know, I'm a mentor to her brother on the weekends and he works for me. I haven't done anything sexual with Diamond," Quentin explained.

"Then why the fuck was you looking at her like that? Like she crossed the line by being here with another nigga?" she questioned.

"Because—" he stopped himself, "I'm about to go handle business, I'll be back."

Getting up from the table, Quentin took a few deep breaths before he went to mingle with the party goers. Seeing Diamond fucked his mind up and being questioned by Maya made that shit worse. He figured a little business talk would make him feel better, but that wasn't the case at all.

As he conversed with his friends and associates, Quentin kept his eyes on Diamond throughout the night. Every time she laughed or smiled at something her date said, he looked to see if it was similar to the way he made her laugh and smile on their date, and it wasn't. When she was with him, Diamond's smiles damn near met her eyes causing them to squint. Knowing that her date didn't have the same affect on her as he did, eased Quentin's mind a little bit. Minutes later, Quentin spotted Diamond and Jordan going to the restroom. Excusing himself from his conversation, Quentin discreetly headed in that direction while Taj and Kyle engaged in conversation. He posted up on the wall outside of the ladies' bathroom, so he wouldn't miss her. When the duo came out of the bathroom laughing, their laughter instantly stopped at the sight of Quentin.

"Jay, do you mind if I talk to Diamond for a moment?"

"Sure. Come find me when you're done, D,"

"Okay."

When Jordan was out of sight, they stared at each other for a moment before he spoke.

"You couldn't give a nigga a heads up that you were gonna be here?" Quentin stepped towards her.

"I coulda, but I didn't feel as though I had to since you didn't invite me," she shrugged.

"So, this is the game you're playing, Diamond?"

"No. Is this the game *you're* playing, Quentin?" she spoke aggressively.

"What you talking about?"

"We had a wonderful date that was filled with laughter, good food and great conversation. You tell me you want to get to know me and see where things go, but I don't hear from you in a week. I know you've never had to work hard to get any woman but that doesn't give you the right to treat me however you want to, and expect me to wait around for you. That's not me. If you really want me, you're gonna have to put some work in and that's the bottom line. And if you're not willing to do that, then lose my damn number."

He could tell that Diamond was waiting for response, but the answer got caught in his throat. When Quentin didn't answer, she walked off, leaving him standing there.

"Fuck!" he cussed out loud before heading back to the main room.

When he made it back to his table, Quentin removed his check book from his inside coat pocket and made the check out for his usual amount before giving it Taj to put in the donation box. Saying good night to his brother and Jordan, he told Kamaya it was time to go and then exited the building without saying a word to each other. The entire ride home to Maya's condo, the car was silent. Both of them were in their own thoughts and feelings. Pulling in the parking lot of her complex, Quentin put the car in park.

"Quentin, I'm—"

"Maya, I need to tell you something and I need you to listen real good, aight?"

"Okay," she nervously replied.

"I appreciate everything you've done for me over the past few years. I don't think I coulda elevated my businesses to the next level without you, but as far as us being sexual, that shit ends tonight."

"What?"

"We can no longer be fuck buddies and business partners. The emotions and feelings that we caught for each other is hurting the business aspect of our relationship, and in order for us to continue doing business together, we have to stop and go back to the way things were," Quentin answered in a serious tone.

"Is this about what happened tonight, because if I it is, I apologize,' Maya pleaded.

"It's not about what happened tonight. I just don't want to keep leading you on like we got a future together and we don't. You're a trill ass chick Maya, and you deserve a nigga that's gonna respect and treat you like a queen. I can't make you my girl because I don't want you to be my girl. I got feelings for someone else."

"How the fuck you just gonna sit up here and tell me you got feelings for someone else and you know how I fucking feel about you, Boss!" she screamed as the tears streamed down her face, and her fist went flying towards his. "I turned down nigga after nigga…. telling myself that you were gonna wife me one day! I was actually waiting on you to make me your girl and you tell me you got feelings for someone else? Fuck you!"

Quentin blocked Kamaya's punches as he leaned up against the driver side door. He let her tire herself out and when she was finished, she got out of the car and took her shoes off. When he peeped that she was about to throw her heels at his truck, Quentin quickly shifted the car in reverse and backed up enough to turn the car around and drive out of the lot. As he headed home, Quentin felt like shit for hurting Maya. He knew that things weren't going to be the same between them and that was a chance that he was willing to take to be with Diamond. He would rather Kamaya know the truth now than for her to find out later. Quentin was ready to show Diamond that he was serious about her and that meant the he needed to put his best foot forward.

CHAPTER 12

Taj and Jordan entered her house hand and hand. He secured the door as Jordan stood in the middle of her living room, unzipping her off the shoulder gown and letting it fall to the floor. Taj licked his lips seductively before walking over to her and kissing her passionately. Taj allowed her to undress him as their tongues wildly danced around each other's mouths. Removing Jordan's strapless nude colored bra, he massaged her 38C breasts before taking the right one into his mouth, causing a small moan to escape her lips. He licked and slurped her nipple like it was his favorite piece of candy. Using his free hand to slip her thong to the side, Taj inserted two fingers inside of her, making Jordan squirm.

"Damn. You dripping wet already and I ain't even taste you yet," he groaned placing his fingers in her mouth.

Jordan licked his fingers clean and he bit his bottom lip at the sight. Standing there naked, Taj back pedaled Jordan to the leather as their tongues danced some more before getting into the sixty-nine position. Taj ripped her thong before tossing the thin fabric on the floor. He spread her pussy lips apart, then dove into her pussy while Jordan went to town on his nine-and-a-half-inch shaft. Taj's tongue and lips had her going crazy as Jordan moaned to the high heavens and tried not to run. His head game was so good that she had to stop sucking and just enjoy the pleasure that she was receiving. Feeling her legs shake, Taj knew that she was on the brink of exploding. He kept that same speed as Jordan rode his face.

"Baby...baby...ooooo!" she screamed as she came all over his face.

Climbing off of him, Jordan quickly sat on his stiff dick and slowly began to ride. Taj pulled her down on top of him and kissed her so she could taste her juices. Bouncing her ass on his dick, Jordan broke their kiss to look into his eyes as she did her thing. Even though no words were exchanged, their intense stare and their moans said it all. Taj never thought that he would allow himself to get close to another female after the betrayal of his ex, but within a week of talking to Jordan, she had him open.

Standing at 6'3", Taj had the muscular built of an athlete. His deep brown, bright eyes and his swag attracted all types of thirst buckets. Unlike his brother, Taj never like the bitches that were willing to give up the coochie easily. He always enjoyed the chase and the challenge, and Jordan was just that. Although she had piqued his interest early, Taj still moved with caution because he didn't want to fall for her too quickly and get played again, but everything played out perfectly. They conversed on the phone for about two weeks straight before they even had their first date, and they didn't have sex until the fifth one. The three and a half months they'd been together was nothing short of amazing, and even though neither one of them uttered the words, they knew that they loved each other and that's what her eyes told him.

Wrapping his arms around her small frame, Taj began to match her rhythm with deep, forceful strokes.

"Yeesss Daddy," Jordan moaned, "Go deep in this pussy."

Obeying her command, he continued to thrust deep inside her as she placed her hands on his chest, arched her back and rode his dick. Their moans, pants, screams and groans grew louder the closer they came to their climax.

"Damn girl! I'm about to nut!"

"So am I!"

Bouncing harder on his dick, Taj gripped her hips tightly, releasing his seed inside her while Jordan's juices covered his dick and lower abdomen. Taking a moment to catch their breath, Taj kissed her forehead when she got comfortable on his chest.

"Damn. That shit was bomb as fuck, bae," she softly moaned.

"Yeah it was. You take this dick like a G, shawty," Taj chuckled.

"Thank you," Jordan giggled. "That was a perfect way to end the perfect evening."

"Yeah it was," he sighed.

The dark room filled with silence as they listened to each other breathe. Feeling Jordan take a long deep breath, Taj felt that something was on her mind.

"Wassup?"

"How much longer are you gonna be staying in the hotel? You been staying in Philly for the past four months and you still haven't found a place yet," she pointed out.

"I stay in hotels because I don't reside in Philly. The entire time we've been talking, I've been commuting back and forth from Baltimore, Jay," he calmly answered.

"I never knew that," she leaned up to look at him. "I thought you resided here?"

"I grew up and resided here until I met my ex, but when

her job relocated her to Baltimore, I got tired of commuting and we moved in together," Taj sighed. "For the past month, I've been trying to decide what to do."

"Well, what do you want to do?"

"I've been thinking about opening up another construction business in Philly so I don't have to close my business in Baltimore, and find a house or a condo here."

"What's stopping you?"

Taj stared into her eyes and with the moonlight shining through the closed blinds, he saw the sad expression displayed on her face.

"You miss your ex, don't you?" Jordan asked softly.

Taj didn't respond. He watched Jordan as she got up and moved to the other side of the couch and folded her arms. Sitting up himself, he tried to find the right words to express how he felt.

"Jay, I spent six years with my ex. I thought she was the love of my life until she cheated on me and got pregnant with another man's baby. That shit hurt like hell and damn near broke me. I left my family and the life I had in Philly behind to be with her, and for her to do me like that had me ready to kill somebody." He paused. "It took me a year to get over her but I didn't start dating until six months after that, and then I meet you and you got a nigga ready to put a ring on ya finger and I've only you known you for three and a half months."

Jordan softly laughed.

"I don't miss my ex, Jordan, and I know I'm gonna sound soft for saying this shit, but I just don't wanna be hurt again," Taj admitted. "I love you Jordan and if I you hurt me, you might as well dig a grave because I might kill ya ass," he seriously spoke.

"I guess you might as well dig one, too, if you hurt me," she moved closer to him, "because I don't play about mine and now that you have my heart, I'm not playing with you either," Jordan confessed unfazed by his threat. "So, are you in this for the long haul?"

Staring deep into her eyes, everything in him told Taj that being with Jordan was the right move to make. He sealed the deal with a kiss before they embraced each other tightly.

"I love you too, Taj Marks," she kissed his neck. "Let's go upstairs so we can start round two."

"Aight, let me grab a couple of bottles of water then I'll be up," he pecked her lips.

As she made her way upstairs, Taj heard his phone vibrating in his pants pocket. Lifting his pants off the floor, he found his phone and answered when he saw it was one of his street employees.

"Yo, Redz. What you find out?"

"That's him. That's the nigga that hit our shit a few years ago. I didn't recognize him at first because he's older and rocking a goatee now, but that's definitely the nigga."

"I knew that motherfucker looked familiar," Taj stormed off to the kitchen so Jordan wouldn't hear him. "That nigga hit plenty of licks over the years. Then he falls off the face of the earth for a few years and resurfaces as a legit businessman. That nigga is smart," he chuckled. "And because he doesn't have a record, my brother doesn't know the type of nigga he is and what he's about."

"What do you want me to do with him, T? I got eyes on that nigga right now. He's leaving the club."

"Follow him. I wanna know where that nigga rests his head at night, as well as the rest of the moves he's making. I need him alive for now and if he wants to do this shit the hard way when I approach him with my brother, then we can murk his ass."

"I'm on it."

Taj ended the call and his blood instantly began to boil. He couldn't believe that the nigga that fucked up his drug deal years ago was running his brother's business. Even though he wanted that fucker alive, Taj was ready to put a bullet through his dome.

When he was heavy in the drug game, Taj was the major supplier of work on the west side of Baltimore. He had his whole drug operation running like clock work for years until Banks killed his connect and his employees and stole the money that Taj had brought to pay for the drugs. He'd always been careful when it came to the moves he made and always double checked to see if niggas were trailing him, but he fucked up with that nigga. The only reason he made it out alive was because he shot Banks twice before he could shoot him. Although Taj slowed him down, that didn't stop Banks from running away. He chased him around the outside of the abandoned warehouse, watching him climb into his car. Banks stared at Taj as he sped off and he never forgot his face.

Grabbing the bottles of water from the fridge, Taj thought about how he was going to explain this shit to Quentin. His brother and Banks had built a bond with each other and he probably considered Banks a friend, but when Taj revealed his past, he knew Quentin wasn't going to want any parts of him because of his background. Hoping for a positive outcome, Taj was also prepared for the negative.

CHAPTER 13

It was a week before the grand opening of the club and Bashir was feeling like he was on top of the world. He'd been working around the clock to get the club ready for its grand opening and trying to prove to Boss that he didn't make a mistake with putting him in charge. Boss approved most of the ideas he had for the club and when he didn't, he privately discussed with Bashir why his idea wouldn't work and not embarrass him in front the employees. Bashir liked the way thatBoss handled business and tried to follow his lead when it came to the club. Bashir believed if he kept grinding like he'd been doing, that Boss would let him fully own the club one day, but he had a feeling that that was only wishful thinking.

Although things were going well on the business front, his personal life was a different story. His life at home with his fiancée was great, but the nightmares that he started having about his old life a few weeks back had Bashir a little paranoid. Whenever he was riding around in the streets, he felt like someone was tailing him. He would pull over on the side of the road or turn down a side block to see if someone followed behind, but they never did. Bashir never spotted any suspicious vehicles with tinted windows or anything like that. So, he was constantly questioning why he felt the way he did.

After spending the morning at the club, Bashir was looking forward to having lunch with Boss. He was caught off guard when he received a text asking Bashir to join him at the *Chickies and Pete's* in South Philly at noon. When he agreed to join him, he felt good about meeting up with him, but that feeling seemed to fade when he hopped in his car making his way to the restaurant.

Bashir arrived ten minutes before noon and spotted Boss leaning against his truck. Parking in the spot, he killed the engine, hopped out his truck and greeted him with a handshake. They made small take about their well being as they entered the restaurant. As soon as the host saw them, he escorted them to a booth in the back. Handing them a menu, the host headed back to the front leaving them alone. They scanned their menus before setting them to the side. Normally, whenever Bashir was scheduled to link up with Boss, he was cool, calm and collected, but since they sat down, he wasn't feeling the vibe that Boss was giving off. Tired of the intense stare down they were having, Bashir broke the silence.

"Aye, I could be wrong, but I feel like something is off about you," he spoke in a deep voice.

"Look Banks, I ain't gonna lie to you," Boss leaned forward, "For the past week and some change, I've been trying to figure why I feel like you haven't been keeping shit a hundred with me."

Swallowing the lump in his throat, Bashir folded his hands on the table and tried his best to remain calm.

"What makes you say that?"

"That's what I'm trying to figure out," he paused, "I've mentioned your name to a few people that I know and they claim they don't know you, but when they see you, they know very well who you are, and what they have to say about you ain't good."

"Whoever you mentioned my name to shouldn't know anything about me, because I don't really know too many in the business industry. They probably have me confused with someone else," Bashir confidently stated.

"I never said that the people who knew you were in the business industry," he replied harshly.

The fact that he knew what Boss was implying caused him to tense up a little. Bashir's heart was beating out of his chest, but he never let his fear show on the outside.

"So what are you trying to say?"

"It doesn't take a rocket scientist to figure out what I'm trying to say, but if you want me to ask, I will. Are you or have you ever been involved with the streets in any way, shape or form?" Boss asked with irritation in his voice.

Bashir parted his lips to answer, but he was cut off.

"Let me say this before you answer. You told me when we first met that you never had affiliation with the streets and that you fell on hard times and needed a hand up. I'm giving you a chance to come clean because if I find out otherwise, I'm gonna be more than pissed that you lied to me, because I vouched for you and stuck my neck out for you. So, think twice before you answer," Boss warned.

The two men stared at each other as Bashir debated with how he wanted to answer Boss. He couldn't believe that his nightmare of his past catching up with him was coming true. He had worked hard to escape the life that he once lived and he'd be damned if he let anyone fuck up the opportunity that was presented to him.

"No," he lied, "I've never been a part of any street activities in my past and I'm not involved in any now," Bashir spoke with a straight face looking him dead in his eyes.

As Boss continued to stare at him, Bashir had a feeling that he didn't believe him and he felt like if he tried to say anything to back up his story, it would only make things worse. The fact that he had lied to Boss again after he presented him with the opportunity to set things right, made Bashir feel like things weren't going to end well for him.

"Aight Banks," Boss nodded, "If that's your story, all I can do is run with it."

"So, we're good now?"

"Yeah. We're straight," Boss stood to his feet. "I hate to run off like this, but I gotta go check on the salon to see how the remodeling is going. I'll be by the club in a couple days to check on things."

"Aight, man," Banks extended his hand for a handshake.

Shaking hands, he watched as Boss made his way out the restaurant. Bashir waited a few minutes before leaving then headed to his car. He spotted a folded piece of paper on his windshield and snatched it off when he reached his truck. Unfolding the paper, the words "You're A Dead Man" was written in marker in bold letters. Observing his surroundings, Bashir didn't see anything out of the ordinary and Boss's truck was nowhere in sight. Hopping inside his truck, he brought it to life and pulled out of the lot. Being as though he just screwed shit up with Boss, Bashir figured he might as well ride this out for as long as he could. Although Boss was the main suspect on his list, he didn't believe that he was the only one gunning for him. If his past had caught up to him, any one of his old enemies could've gotten wind of his whereabouts and where he lived. Thinking of Morgan and Marie, Bashir felt his heart sink to his feet at the thought of his family getting killed behind his past sins. He tried his best to adapt to his new life and he kept his inner savage tucked away for a few years, but he was willing to go back to his savage ways if it meant him saving himself and his family.

CHAPTER 14

When the weekend rolled around, Quentin was looking forward to hanging with the young bucks. Since he'd been mentoring the boys for nearly two months, he'd grown attached to them. Quentin felt like they were his little brothers instead of his mentees. Even though Riko was his family, he treated Justin like his family as well, and he treated them both equally. They'd been working well together at the clothing store and since they started working there, their sales had increased. Quentin liked how the boys attracted teenagers to the store and they became his regular customers. He noticed how Riko flirted with most of the young female customers that came through, while Justin just stuck to his job. Riko and Justin were like day and night, but Quentin believed that they balanced each other out.

Walking to the front of the store, Quentin noticed that Justin was having a conversation with a girl and an older woman while Riko dealt with a customer. He headed over to him and cleared his throat.

"Hello Ma'am, is everything okay here?" He stood on the left side of Justin.

"Yes sir. Everything is fine, I just wanted to meet the young man that's taking my daughter out this evening. We were in the area and Kailyn mentioned that he worked here. So, we stopped in for a visit," the lady explained.

"I understand ma'am," he nodded his head. "I'm Quentin. Justin's boss and mentor." He extended his hand to her.

"Nice to meet you. I'm Georgia. Kailyn's mother," she shook his hand, "Will you be chaperoning their date, tonight?"

"No ma'am. My sister, Diamond, will be chaperoning us this evening. You'll meet her when we come to pick up Kailyn," Justin answered.

"Very well. We have to go now. We'll see you later, Justin, and don't be late," Georgia pointed at him.

"Yes ma'am," Justin smiled.

"See you later Justin," Kailyn gave him a quick hug before jogging out of the store.

"Okay Jus! I see you man," Quentin teased. "You got ya first date tonight, huh?"

"Yeah and I'm nervous. I mean, I always hang with Kailyn at school and we catch the bus together, but we've never been alone. Like by ourselves."

"Oh I see," Quentin rubbed his chin hair. "Well come see me when your shift is over and we'll talk."

"Aight."

Heading to his office, Quentin took a seat behind his desk, snatched his phone up and began calling Diamond on FaceTime. For the past week, they'd been talking everyday and as much as he enjoyed talking to her, he cussed himself for not pursuing Diamond sooner. When the call connected, he was greeted by her beautiful, smiling face.

"Wassup gorgeous?" He licked his lips.

"Nothing much, Handsome. Wassup with you?"

"I just met Justin's date and her mom. They came to the store to see him."

"Oh really?"

"Yeah. Kailyn's mother wanted to meet the young man who was taking her daughter out. They left about five minutes ago."

"This should be interesting," she chuckled.

"Why you didn't tell me you were chaperoning Justin's date tonight?"

"Because you've had my little brother to yourself every weekend for the past month and some change, and I wanted to see him on his first date," she answered. "To be honest, I thought he might've asked you but when he asked me last week, I couldn't say no."

"Awww you miss ya lil brother huh?" He chuckled.

"Yes I do," Diamond smiled. "But to be honest, I don't know what I'm gonna do while they're playing video games and stuff at Dave and Buster's. I need a date of my own."

"What happened to ol' boy from the Gala?" he snidely asked.

"Kyle is just my co-worker. Nothing more. Nothing less. He needed a date for the event. He asked. I accepted. End of story," she answered honestly.

"That's all it better be. Don't get homeboy fucked up," Quentin's toned turned serious.

"I know you're not jealous, Quentin Marks," Diamond teased.

"I don't get jealous," he huffed.

"Good, because he doesn't have anything on you," she winked. "So, will you be my date for the night? With you being there, it might help Jus relax and not be so nervous."

"I was gonna pop up anyway but now that you asked, I don't have to stalk y'all," he laughed and so did she.

"Aight, you can meet us at the Dave and Buster's at

Franklin Mills. I'm picking Kailyn up at seven and she has to be home by ten."

"That's cool. I'll see you there."

"Bye," she smiled before ending the call.

Placing the phone on the desk, Quentin couldn't help the grin that appeared on his face. Diamond had him feeling like a teenager who won a date with the most popular girl in school. He had never felt that way in all of his twenty-eight years of living. All of the females that he came across were the same. When he introduced himself to a woman, their eyes seemed to light up and their panties got wet at the thought of being with a boss. They thought all they had to do was fuck him like a porn star to earn the main spot on his team, but little did they know, it took more than that to get to his heart, which was something Quentin had never given to any woman. He felt that love was one of the worst ways for a woman to make a fool out of man and vice versa. He had seen his share of failed relationships where a man was cheating on a good woman, or a woman just stayed with a man for bread, just to leave when he lost it all; and where a woman would have a nigga so in love with her that he couldn't see through the signs and the lies that she was fucking every nigga that crossed her path. Quentin couldn't understand why people played a fool just to say that they loved someone, and the shit wasn't genuine. He'd be damned if he let a bitch play him like that, but the way Diamond had him feeling after only a week of talking and one date, had Quentin contemplating about having a relationship with shawty.

A knock on the door brought him back to reality and when he saw it was Taj, he stood to his feet to greet him with a brief hug.

"I wasn't expecting to see you today," He spoke once he was back behind his desk.

"I know, but I needed to talk to you about something important," Taj took a seat in the office chair.

"If it's about Banks, I already know," Quentin gazed at his brother. "What I can't understand is why you didn't tell me about him."

"When I first saw him on the monitor, I wasn't sure if that was him but I told a couple of my boys to post up outside of the club and wait for him to make an appearance to see if that was him, and they verified that he's the nigga that robbed me a few years back," he balled his fist up as he spoke. "I wasn't trying to keep shit from you, bro. I just wanted to make sure he was the right nigga."

"I can understand that," he nodded. "When that nigga first came to me, he fed me some bullshit story about him being down on his luck and he wanted to try his hand at being an entrepreneur. After I did a background check on him and saw that he was clean, I took him under my wing. Banks never gave off the vibe like he was lying because you know I can see through that shit, but maybe the sign was there and I chose to ignore it. I don't know. Anyway, a week or so after I put him in charge of the barbershop, someone sent shots through the shop. No one was hurt, but my employees were telling me that he was the reason for the shooting, but I didn't want to believe it. I met with him this week to give him a chance to come clean, but he lied to me again and I can't let that shit slide. Not a second time," Quentin spoke with anger.

"This nigga must have a death wish, man," Taj stood to his feet starting to pace. "I'm ready to handle this nigga right now!"

"I feel you bro and I wanna be there when you do," his tone turned serious.

"I can't let you do that, Q," Taj shook his head, "You got too much to lose. You got ya businesses, you're a mentor and you and Diamond are finally hitting off. You know how street niggas are. They used to let women and children live but now, they'll off them, too, and not give a fuck. Riko and Justin don't need a target on their back and neither does Diamond," he stopped pacing. "You retired from the streets years ago and reinvented yaself. Don't go back and risk losing everything you worked so hard for," Taj pleaded.

"But you got shit to lose, too, T."

"Yeah but this shit is personal for me. I had to fight for my damn life for like a year after that stunt Banks pulled. Word got back that my connect got popped in a robbery and them motherfuckers came out of the woodworks to kill my ass." He walked over to his desk. "My business is in Baltimore and I don't have a residence here, but I will when all this bullshit is over. So, for the last time, please let me handle Banks," Taj pleaded.

Taking a moment to think, Quentin couldn't deny that everything his brother said was true. All Banks did was lie to his face twice but the shit that Taj had to go through after Banks robbed them pissed him off the same way it did back then. Quentin wanted to rush to his brother's aid to help him, but Taj insisted on handling things himself and he survived. Although he put the street shit behind him, Quentin was ready to bust his gun just to make an example out of Banks, but thinking of all he had to lose and the promise he made to Diamond to keep Justin safe, Quentin couldn't allow himself to return to the bloody and crime filled life he'd left behind.

"Okay," he stood to his feet, "But when you get him, make sure that nigga is dead before you take off. You hear me?"

"No doubt," Taj stood up tall. "When do you want this handled?"

"Anytime between now and Thursday. The grand opening is Friday and I can't have him there as the face of my club."

"Say no more. I'll make sure that shit is over with quick."

Quentin came around his desk and gave his brother a quick hug, then he watched Taj storm out his office like a man on a mission. Although he was worried about his brother's safety, there was no doubt in Qunetin's mind that Taj was going to be victorious in this battle.

"Aye Boss, I'm about to head home so I can get ready for my date," Justin peeked his head in after he knocked.

"Cool and you don't have anything to worry about because I'm gonna be there to guide you and make sure you have some alone time with Kailyn," he smirked.

"For real?"

"Yup. Your sister invited me out with y'all tonight."

"Wait a minute," Justin entered the office. "You talking to my sister?"

"We're just friends Jus," Quentin explained.

"So you're the one she went out with last weekend?"

"Nah. The week before. Last weekend she went out with some clown," he shook his head, "I don't even wanna get into that."

Justin stared at him with a stone face and didn't speak a word.

"You aight, man?"

"We'll talk about this later," Justin huffed, "I gotta go."

After Justin quickly left the office, Quentin stood in the middle of it, confused. He didn't understand why Justin acted that way towards him about dating his sister, but he was going to make sure he got to the bottom of it. Putting his issue with Justin to the back of his mind, Quentin snatched up Riko and headed home to get ready for his evening with Diamond.

* * *

AFTER SPENDING thirty minutes helping her brother decide on an outfit, Diamond and Justin headed out the apartment. Locking the door behind her, they headed out the building and hopped into her freshly detailed and washed car. The month of April was near and the Spring weather was still on the chilly side, but not freezing.

"Dang sis," Justin looked around admiring the car. "You didn't have to do all this for my date."

"Yes, I did," she started the car, "this is your first date and I didn't want your lil girl friend to think I was dirty and I wanted to set an example of how your car should look when you're going to be escorting people, especially a female around, aight?"

"Aight," he chuckled.

"Cool. Now let's ride."

Pulling out of the lot, Diamond headed to the Nicetown Section of Philly to pick up Kailyn. She lived down the street from Gratz Hight School which was the school they both attended. As Meek Mills song 'Dangerous' came through speakers, she glanced over at her brother and saw that he wasn't as happy as he was when they left.

"You look like you're in deep thought over there. What's on your mind?"

"Boss told me that he'll be joining us tonight. Is that true?"

"Yes. I invited him so he could keep me company while you and Kailyn get to know one another. Is that a problem?"

Justin took a moment to respond.

"I wouldn't say it's a problem. I know Boss is a good dude, but he's not relationship material. He's a playa for real, and I don't want that type of man dating my sister," Justin sternly spoke.

"Justin, do you think I would really be giving Q the time of day if I didn't expect him to do right by me?"

"I know you wouldn't."

"I went out on a date with Q two weeks ago and the date was perfect. At the end I gave him my number and he didn't call me until a week later. It took for him to see me out with another man for him to get his act together because I told him that if he wasn't willing to put the work in to be with me, then he needed to lose my number. The next day, Q called me and told me that he was willing to do whatever it took for us to work," Diamond smirked.

"Dang. For real?" Justin gasped.

"Yup," she nodded. "Men respect women on how they carry themselves. If women are easily giving up the pussy, then they're not gonna respect them very much because if she's quick to give it up to one man, she'll be quick to give it up to the next; but women who make men respect them and carry themselves like ladies and not ho's get treated like a queen and more times than none, they get the ring," Diamond pulled down Kailyn's block. "I appreciate you looking out for me but just know, ya sister got this," she winked.

"Aight sis," he grinned.

"Now let's go get your date."

They hopped out the car and Justin jogged onto the porch, ringing the doorbell while Diamond waited at the bottom of the steps. When the door opened, Kailyn and her mother stepped outside to greet them. She introduced herself to Kailyn's mother, Georgia and she complimented Justin on his outfit. Georgia pointed out that they were matching with their red shirts, light denim jeans and their black and red Jordan's. The couple blushed. Saying their good-byes to Georgia, the women watched as Justin opened the back door for Kailyn before getting in the back with her. Taking her place behind the wheel, Diamond drove down the small block and headed towards the expressway.

As Diamond drove through the Northeast, she glanced in

the backseat to see how her brother was doing, and they seemed to be getting along just fine. They started out on opposite ends of the car but some how managed to be sitting in the middle next to each other when they reached the mall. Diamond was impressed with Kailyn's knowledge of sports and she overheard Kailyn's plans of attending Norfolk State University and studying criminal justice or business when she graduated high school in a couple of years.

They arrived at the Franklin Mills Mall forty-five minutes later. Diamond had to drive around the parking lot a few times to find a parking spot because it was packed. Killing the engine, she hopped out the car in time to see her brother help his date out of the car. Impressed by Justin's gentleman-like behavior, Diamond had a feeling that Quentin had given him some pointers of what to do on his date. Making their way to the front door, she spotted Quentin waiting for them and she couldn't control her smile.

"Hello beautiful," he extended his arms to hug her.

"Hey you," she wrapped her arms around him. "Don't you look handsome," Diamond admired his outfit.

"Don't get me started on you," Quentin licked his lips, making her blush.

"Excuse me y'all," Justin interrupted. "We're gonna go inside and play some games. Is that cool with y'all?"

"Yeah, that's fine. Y'all have fun," Diamond smiled.

They watched as Justin held the door open for Kailyn before Quentin held the door for her.

"So, how's he doing so far?" he asked.

"Surprisingly well. He's been opening doors for that girl all night. I think her mother was impressed, too. I guess it's safe to say that you had something to do with that?"

Quentin smirked.

When Quentin guided her over to one of the many pool tables, she raised an eyebrow at him.

"Uh, what are you doing?" She stood off to the side.

"Setting up the pool table," he answered nonchalantly. "You play, don't you?"

"I used to play quite a bit when I was a teenager, but that was years ago," she hung her purse on the rack and grabbed a stick.

"Let me see what you got first and if you need coaching, I'll help you," he winked.

Removing the rack from the balls, Diamond watched Quentin as he chalked up his stick. The Polo Red cologne he was wearing smelled damn good and was making her maintain her composer around him. He took the first hit, sending the pool balls flying in every direction, but none of them went in. Making her way to the table, Diamond got in position to take her shot and sent one of the striped balls flying into the left corner pocket. She caught Quentin's reaction to her shot and smiled to herself. After making all of the striped balls disappear in the pockets, Diamond got in position to sink the eight ball in the side pocket and just like the others, it went in with ease.

"That's game," she smiled.

"I can't believe this," Quentin stared at her in disbelief. "You hustled me."

"I didn't hustle you, I told you I haven't played in years and you assumed that I was trash, but I proved that ass wrong, didn't I?" she smirked.

"Aight. Well if you think you got skills like that, put ya money where your mouth is," he tossed two C-notes on the table.

"Rack 'em up," Diamond tossed her money on the table.

After removing the rack, Quentin took the first shot sending two of the striped balls flying into the corner pockets. He made two consistent shots and Diamond was starting to get nervous. As she stood at the opposite end of the table,

Diamond purposely dropped her money on the floor behind her. Just as Quentin was about to take his shot, she bent over to pick up the money, giving him a clear view of her round ass making him scratch. After he accused her of foul play, Diamond grabbed her stick and sunk all the solid balls into the pockets, winning the game and the money. As she fanned herself with the money she won, Quentin strolled away without saying a word and Diamond couldn't control her laughter.

Once she caught up to Quentin, she was about to call her brother to ask him if they were ready to eat, but when she spotted Justin with a frown on his face and Kailyn grinning from ear to ear, Diamond knew that Kailyn had beaten him.

"You lost to huh?" she chuckled.

"Kailyn cheated," Justin mumbled.

"So did ya sister," Quentin gave her the side eye. "She beat me outta two-hundred dollars."

"Kailyn beat me outta one-fifty," he glared at her.

"I told you I was nice when it came to hoops, but you underestimated me," Kailyn shrugged.

"The girls are dominating tonight."

The girls gave each other a high five which irritated the men. After spending a couple of minutes gloating, the two couples found an empty table, so they could eat. Once the waiter had taken their orders, they conversed about anything that came to mind and the more Diamond found out about Kailyn, the more she like her. After filling up on wings, burgers, fries and drinks, the couples decided to play a game of bowling, so the men could redeem themselves. It was girls vs boys and even though the girls decided to let them win, they ended up winning the game because the men were just that terrible. After losing most of the night, Quentin and Justin were ready to go and they needed to get Kailyn home before her curfew. Once they were in their cars, Diamond pulled out of the spot and notice that Quentin was following her.

Arriving at Kailyn's house a half hour later, Diamond noticed that she was resting on Justin's shoulder with his arm around her. Lightly shaking her awake, he helped Kailyn out of the car and guided her up the steps. Before her mother answered the door, she kissed Justin's cheek and gave him the money back she won. Saying good night to Georgia, Justin hopped in the passenger seat of Quentin's truck. As she headed over to her car where Quentin was waiting for her, they embraced each other in a hug and Diamond was caught off guard when he shoved his tongue in her mouth. A part of her wanted to pull away, but the passion she felt from him allowed her to fall deep into the kiss. They got lost in each other until they were interrupted by Justin honking the car horn.

"Let me know when you make it home, aight?"

"Okay," Diamond answered in shock.

They exchanged a quick look before Quentin opened the car door for her, closing it once she was inside. Diamond drove down the block and headed home with Quentin on her mind the entire time. The kiss they shared had Diamond wanting more. It had been awhile since she had any affection from a man, and the only pleasure she received was from her vibrator that she kept hidden in her nightstand. Diamond was trying to hold out from having sex with Quentin until she felt he deserved it, but she felt like he wasn't going to be able to hold out too much longer.

CHAPTER 15

When Monday rolled around, Kamaya sat in the parking lot of the Boss's office building debating on what to do with the envelope she had in her hand. It was her letter of resignation that she'd written in the past week. Since he cut her off the weekend before, Kamaya had been M.I.A., and what made things even worse was that Boss didn't even call to make sure she was still breathing. She tried to convince herself that she could continue to work with Boss without having any hard feelings or not wanting to be sexual, but she was only lying to herself. Kamaya was in love with Boss and she couldn't handle being just his business partner.

Getting out of the car, she caught the elevator to the fifteenth floor and since it was still the seven o' clock hour, the building was still empty. The only person there was the receptionist.

"Good Morning. Can you make sure that Boss gets this, please?" Kamaya handed the receptionist her envelope.

"I sure will," the receptionist responded with a smile.

Turning on her heels, she took the elevator down to the main floor, hopped in her car and drove off heading towards her house. When she arrived home, Kamaya locked herself in her room, flopped down on her bed and cried, but she didn't know if she was crying out of hurt or anger. She replayed the night in her head where Quentin told her that he had feelings for someone else. Boss's words ripped through her heart causing it to shatter instantly. Despite their business accomplishments, Kamaya thought the chemistry between them was mutual. She thought they shared the same feelings and being as though she was able to keep her mouth shut for weeks about the women he was fucking, her mission to capture Boss's heart was a complete bust.

In the mix of her crying, Kamaya dozed off to sleep. The back to back text messages she received woke her up from her sleep. Slowly sitting up on her bed, she grabbed her phone and checked it. She had two missed calls from Boss and she was about to call him to see what he wanted but she checked the texts she received, instead. Anger boiled inside her as she looked at pictures of Boss and the girl from the Gala having either lunch or dinner together. Kamaya couldn't believe that Boss had passed her over for a basic bitch like her. Scrolling down the thread, she read the text underneath the pictures.

Unknown: Are you ready to join me now?

Studying the message, she thought about who could've sent it to her. Thinking back to the conversation she had with Garrick, the wheels in her head began turning. Although she was aware of his history, Kamaya thought of Garrick's positive traits. He had all of the qualities of a hustler and with her help, she felt as though as she could help him reach his full potential. Calling the number, Kamaya waited for him to answer.

"I see you got the messages I sent you," he snidely said.

"Yes I did, and I decided to join you," Kamaya replied.

"Great," he shouted. "Now first things first. I need to you find me an office building. I don't want it to be too close to Center City though, but I still want it to be in a nice area," Garrick ordered, "Oh I need you find out everything you can on Bashir Phillips."

"Who?"

"That nigga Banks that's running that club that's about to open on Friday."

"Oh," she rolled her eyes, "what do you want to know about him for?"

"Listen, I figure that you only want to deal with the business side of things. So leave this street shit alone. Just do what I tell you, and don't ask me any questions unless its business related, aight?"

"Fine."

"Cool. Hit me back when you find something."

Garrick abruptly ended the call, leaving Kamaya confused. She recalled Boss telling her that Banks was legit when he first told her about him. Although she never doubted Boss, she knew something wasn't right about Banks. Kamaya just couldn't prove it, but hearing Garrick mention the streets, she knew that Banks must've been affiliated with them in some form or fashion. Feeling the sudden urge to call Boss, Kamaya didn't know if she should give him a heads up about Banks. Instead of calling him, she shot him a text and he instantly replied.

Boss: I know about Banks, but thanks for the heads up and thank you for the help you've given me over the years. I'm sorry it had to come to this.

Kamaya: I am too, but I wish you well in all your future endeavors, and good luck with the grand opening of the club on Friday.

Feeling her eyes water, Kamaya wiped her eyes before the tears fell. She tossed her phone to the side and grabbed her MacBook Pro and began her investigation on Banks. She was interested to find out who Bashir Phillips really was and what he had to hide.

CHAPTER 16

"What the fuck you mean my services are no longer needed!" Bashir's voice echoed throughout Boss's office "You know how much time I put into getting that fucking club ready?" He stood to his feet.

"Like I said, I appreciate all that you've done for me over the year and making all of the preparations for the club, but I no longer need your services. You are not the type of person I want being associated with my business," Boss boldly stated. "Being as though you were my business partner with venture, I'm prepared to buy you out."

"Fuck that buy out shit, Boss! I want to run the fucking club. I earned that shit!" Bashir fumed. "And what the fuck you mean I'm not the type of person you want associated with your business!"

"Nigga you know what the fuck I'm talking about!" Boss jumped to his feet, pushing his chair back with his leg. "I came to you as a man, business partner and friend and asked you if you had any affiliations with the streets and you lied to my face! Twice! I fucking vouched for you when niggas were coming at me telling me to let ya ass go. My business was shot up and I *still* decided to give you a chance and you still said fuck me! So, you can either take this and leave outta here with some bread, or you can fucking leave here broke. The fucking choice is yours!"

The two were engaged in an intense stare down and Bashir was seeing red. Although Boss was telling the truth and knew some shit like this was going to happen, he wasn't trying to hear it. The fact that he spent the last month working his ass off getting the club ready for business, just for Boss to snatch that shit away from him, was some bullshit.

"I'm not taking shit," he answered through gritted teeth. "I can take ya ass to court behind this shit."

Boss couldn't control his laughter.

"Take me to court and do what? Lose? Ya name ain't on shit. I own *all* of my businesses. Including the club. *My* name is on that fucking building. I put you in position to run it because I felt like you deserved it. I called you my business partner because I wanted you to be on my level and so you could be respected, so when you started running shit on ya own, you wouldn't have any problems with the employees. I did that shit outta the kindness of my heart and to make shit easy because you so called had a bad break and wanted to be an entrepreneur, and you turned around and spit in my fucking face," Boss replied in disgust, "Get the fuck outta my office."

"You won't get away with this shit, Boss. You better believe that," Bashir pointed at him before he left the office.

Storming past a few of the employees, Banks headed straight for the elevator and pushed the down button. Bashir stepped onto the elevator and he became annoyed with the multiple stops it took on the way to the main lobby. Not caring about the rest of the people on the elevator, Bashir bumped through the crowd and was the first one off. Power walking through the lobby, he unlocked his car doors with the remote before hopping inside. Bringing his black 2018 BMW to life, Bashir reached in the glove compartment removing his desert eagle and placing it on his lap. Since his last meeting with Boss, Bashir decided to switch cars because he was being followed. He couldn't make out who was driving because of the tinted windows, but Bashir knew that a car was tailing him. Since he switched cars, the black Chevy Impala was no longer on his trail.

As Bashir waited for Boss to come out of his office, his phone began to ring. He rolled his eyes when he saw that it was Morgan. He didn't want to answer because he didn't want them to continue the argument he walked out on that morning, but Bashir knew that she wasn't going to stop calling until he answered. So, he did.

"Morgan, I ain't got time for this shit right now," he groaned.

"What the fuck you mean you don't have time for this shit right now? I ask you what's going on with you, you tell me that things took a turn for the worst, grab your gun and don't explain to me what the hell is going on. I tell you that if you decide to turn to the streets that I'm gonna leave and you tell me to do what I gotta do? What type of shit is that, Bashir?" Morgan tried to remain calm. "You said that shit like you don't give a fuck about me taking our daughter and leaving."

"Look Morgan," He sighed, "I apologize for being so cold to you this morning. It's just that the nightmares I told you I was having finally came true. Boss asked me to come clean with him about my past and I lied to him, and he fired me. I just left his office and to make shit worse, someone was following me. That's why I don't drive the truck and that's also why I won't let you drive either," Bashir admitted.

"Oh my God, Bashir! Why the fuck wouldn't you tell me

some shit like that?" Morgan shouted, "And why the fuck would you lie to Boss after everything he's done for us. If it wasn't for him helping you, you woulda been stuck in the same mindset and still robbing niggas to make a living. He introduced you to a new life and you done fucked that up!" she sighed.

The phone fell silent as Bashir listened to his fiancée's truthful rant.

"So what are you gonna do now, Bashir?"

"I'm gonna open up my own business," He answered. "I have the knowledge and the experience of how to do this shit and after everything that has happened, it's time for me to do this shit on my own."

"Sounds good to me, but what about this street shit, bae? I don't want anything to happen to you, Bashir. I'd lose my mind without you."

"Don't worry about me, baby. I'll be fine. I'll see you when I get home."

"Okay. I love you and please be careful," Morgan pleaded.

"I love you, too."

Ending the call, Bashir killed the engine and continued to wait for Boss. The phone call with his fiancée pissed him off a little bit because she didn't take his side in the situation with Boss, but at the end of the day, he couldn't blame her. He had fucked up the best opportunity that had ever been presented to him and because Bashir couldn't handle his mistake, he was ready to put an end to Boss.

After waiting on Boss for two hours, Bashir brought his car to life and began to follow him. As he cautiously maneuvered through the streets, he felt that Boss was going to the club because of the direction he was taking. Instead of staying a few cars behind him, he took the back route to the club in hopes of beating him there. There were cameras surrounding the building so Bashir parked in an ally way to avoid being spotted. Killing the engine, he grabbed his gun before getting out the car and popping the trunk. Bashir snatched up his bulletproof vest but before he could put it on, the sound of screeching tires caught his attention, causing him to turn around. Seeing the guns from a car window aimed at him, Bashir quickly tried to take cover but before he could, a barrage of bullets went flying in his direction, hitting him everywhere from his neck, to his legs, causing him to drop to the ground on his stomach. As the blood spilled from his body, he heard footsteps approaching and felt hands on his neck checking for a pulse. Bashir could feel his attacker towering over him and the two shots he fired into his back caused him to pass out instantly.

CHAPTER 17

The grand opening for the club was a bigger success than Quentin could've hoped for and although he was no longer walking the earth, he had to thank Banks and Kamaya for that. It pained him that the two people who helped him get the club up and running were no longer with him, but Quentin knew that he was going to have to push past his loss and find a replacement for Kamaya. He decided to handle the day to day operations for the club, but he needed someone to stay on top of advertising and promoting the club. Everyone from all over came out for the grand opening and he watched as everyone enjoyed themselves from the VIP section with Diamond, Taj, Jordan and a couple of Taj's henchmen gathered around him. When the club closed at two in the morning, Taj and Jordan went their separate ways while Quentin suggested that Diamond stay the night with him. He was expecting her to say no, but when she didn't, he was caught off guard.

When they arrived at his house, Diamond was stunned at how beautiful his home was. Quentin gave her the tour and ended it in the basement where they found Justin playing the game. When Justin saw that his sister was there, he stared at both of them and without saying a word, he turned the game off and went upstairs.

"What the hell is wrong with him?" Diamond asked in confusion.

"I don't know, but I'll go talk to him," he kissed her lips. "In the meantime, why don't you go upstairs and get ready for me," Quentin wrapped his hands around her waist.

"Wait a minute. I agreed to spend the night. That doesn't mean we're having sex," Diamond stated with grin. "I'll be sleeping in the guest room. Just leave one of your shirts for me to sleep in on the bed and I'll be good," she headed up the stairs.

"Damn, that's cold, Diamond," he shook his head, following her up the stairs.

Quentin watched as Diamond dipped off into the bathroom. Stopping in front of Justin's door, he knocked before letting himself in.

"What do you want man," Justin spat.

"Damn. That's how you talk to me now?"

"Yeah," he put the book down that he was reaching. "Since you started dating my sister, I feel left out, now. It used to be just me, you and Riko on the weekends and now it's like y'all got better shit to do besides hang with me. I know I can chill with Kailyn but I see her all the time in school. Sometimes, I just wanna chill with the fellas and the fact that you're dating my sister still doesn't sit right with me," he huffed.

"Why does it bother you? Because you think I'm gonna do your sister wrong?" Quentin stepped closer to him.

"Yeah! If something goes wrong between you and Diamond, what the hell is going to happen to me? Are you still gonna be there for me? Are you gonna treat me differently? Are you gonna fire me?"

Seeing the hurt in his eyes broke Quentin's heart.

Walking over to the desk, he took a seat while Justin sat down on the bed.

"Let me explain something to you, Jus. It took me awhile to muster up the courage to pursue your sister because I knew she was a challenge, and that she wasn't gonna take no shit off me, and she doesn't. I respect your sister and you have my word that I would never do anything to hurt Diamond," he spoke sincerely. "And even if things don't work out with me and your sister, my relationship with you ain't gonna change. I was cool with you before I even went on a date with Diamond. I know the role I play in yours and Riko's lives being as the though y'all don't have male figures to look up to, and the last thing I'm gonna do is abandon y'all. Aight?"

"Aight," Justin nodded.

"Cool. By the way, where is Riko?" Quentin stood to his feet.

"Riko said that he wouldn't be joining us this weekend because he had something to do. He got defensive when I asked what he had to do and when I saw him walk off with one of the dope boys from the neighborhood, I kinda knew what he was gonna do. He's been missing school a lot lately and I think he's starting to sell drugs. I try to talk to him but he doesn't hear me. I'm worried about him, Q."

Hearing the news about Riko filled Quentin with anger, but he didn't let his anger show.

"Don't worry about Riko. I'll handle it, aight?"

"Cool."

They shook hands before Quentin made his way out of the room and headed to his room where he saw Diamond wrapped in a towel, removing a t-shirt from his drawer. When she turned around, he couldn't help the lustful stare that was displayed on face. Smirking at him, Diamond seductively walked over to him.

"Take a cold shower and I'll see you in the morning," she winked at him before leaving his room.

"This girl is driving me the fuck crazy," Quentin ran his hand over his head.

Taking off his suit, dress socks and shoes, he placed them in the closet before putting on a pair of ball shorts and getting in bed with his phone in hand. He called Riko to see if he was going to answer but his phone went all the way through to voicemail. Quentin called him three more times only to get the same response. He found his aunt Kim's name in his phone and called her. He didn't expect her to answer, but she did.

"Quentin, why the hell are you calling me this late at night? What's wrong? Is Riko okay?" she grumbled.

"I was calling to see if Riko was there with you. He didn't show up to work and he didn't come to my house."

"What? When I spoke to him at eight o'clock, he said he was with you and Justin at the house," Kim became frantic. "Oh my God, Quentin! Where the hell is Riko?"

"I don't know, but Justin said that Riko has been missing school and hanging with the neighborhood dope boys. He said he tried to stop him, but Riko left and joined them."

"Oh no! Have you tried calling him?"

"Yeah. He didn't answer. It rang all the way through to voicemail."

"I just checked his room and he's not there! Oh Lord! This can't be happening. I gotta find my son! He's connected to my tracking app. When I find him, I'll give a call," Kim ended the call abruptly.

Worried about Riko, Quentin wanted to rush out the door and search for him too, but he didn't even know where to begin to look. Learning that Riko was hanging in the streets irritated him greatly. He spent every weekend explaining to the boys that it was other ways for them to live their lives instead of being dope boys, stick up kids and an assassin. Quentin took them to different restaurants and shopping malls outside of Philly. He even took them to a few Sixers games because neither of them had ever been. He thought he was making a difference in their lives, but could tell that he needed to work on Riko a little more.

An hour had passed and he still hadn't heard from his aunt. He was fighting his sleep trying to stay up and before he could doze off, the ringing of his cell phone startled him.

"Yo, auntie. Did you find him?"

"Yeah," she cried, "I found him in an alley in South Philly. He was shot a couple of times but he's still breathing. I'm rushing him to Pennsylvania Hospital now."

"Aight auntie. I'll meet you there."

Jumping out of bed, Quentin removed his ball shorts, replacing them with black Nike sweatpants and snatched the matching hoodie from his closet. He slid his feet into his Nike slippers before snatching his phone off the bed and darting out of his room and down the hall to Justin's room.

"Justin! Wake up! We gotta go to the hospital! Riko was shot! Come on! We gotta go!" he shook him awake.

Without hesitation, Justin hopped out of bed searching for his clothes. Leaving the room, Quentin bumped into Diamond in the hallway and he explained to her about Riko before dashing down the stairs and out the door. Starting his truck, he waited a few seconds for Justin before he came running out of the house and jumping into the truck. Quentin backed out of the driveway like a bat out of hell heading towards the expressway. His heart was racing out of his chest as he drove above the speed limit to get to his cousin. He prayed said a silent prayer all the way to the hospital and was ready to kill whoever was responsible for shooting Riko.

* * *

AFTER QUENTIN and Justin left the house, Diamond was on edge and worried about Riko. She had a million and one questions running through her mind. She wanted to know what type of shit that Riko was involved with and if she should cut Justin off from hanging with him. Diamond knew that Riko was Quentin's cousin, but if he was going to be involved in the streets, she didn't want him hanging around Justin by any means. The only problem with that was being as though they were both being mentored by Quentin and they were best friends, it was going to be difficult to keep them separated since they went to school, worked and hung out together.

Tired of looking at the for walls in the guest room, Diamond headed down the hall to Quentin's room and climbed into his huge bed. Turning on the TV, she flipped through the channels until she came across 'Charmed' on TNT. As soon as snuggled under the covers, Diamond was fast asleep. Felling a soft kiss on her forehead, she began to squirm in her sleep.

"Diamond. Wake up baby," Quentin called out to her.

"Mmmmm. I'm up," she stretched, "How's Riko?"

"He's good. They had to surgically remove the bullets from his body, but he pulled through just fine," he gave a small smile.

"That's great. I was so worried about him," Diamond sat up in bed. "Did he say who shot him?"

"Yeah," he sighed, "His friends took him to meet the nigga they were selling drugs for in an ally in South Philly. Some nigga named G told him that he would supply him with some work if he killed me and Justin. When Riko told him no, one of the lil niggas shot him twice and they left him there to die," he answered solemnly.

"Oh my God!"

"I asked him why he started hanging with them in the first place and Riko said that he was tired of being teased for going to class every day and for hanging with a square like Justin. He apologized to me for not listening to the warnings I gave him and I told him that it was okay. I was furious with Riko before I got there but once I saw him, I felt like him being laid up in the hospital was my fault for some reason," Quentin sighed.

"Awww, baby. Don't you go blaming yourself for this mess. Riko made the decision to follow behind the drug dealers instead of staying on the right path which was sticking with you and Justin. This is not your fault, Q," she wrapped her arms around his shoulders. "But why would this nigga G want you and my brother dead? Are you involved in something that I need to know about?" Diamond glared at him.

"No, Diamond" he sternly answered. "I don't know who G is but I'm gonna find out and settle whatever issue he has with me, but you don't have anything to worry about," Quentin assured her.

They stared at each other for a moment before Quentin leaned in and kissed her. Diamond wrapped her arms around his neck, forcing her tongue inside his mouth. Wrapping his arms around her waist, he lifted her up and laid her on her back across the bed. Diamond moaned as he kissed and sucked her neck while his hands slid under the t-shirt she was wearing, caressing her naked body underneath. Diamond allowed him to remove the shirt and Quentin quickly took her left breast into his mouth.

"Q? Baby wait a minute. Where's Justin," she moaned.

"Still at the hospital with Niko and his mom. He wanted to stay. I'm picking him up later."

"Good."

Quentin continued to suck, lick and gently bite her nipple like a newborn baby breastfeeding. Diamond bit her lip as she moaned. The pleasure that he was giving her was long over due, and she was yearning for more. Diamond giggled as he placed kisses down her stomach and when he reached her thighs, Quentin kissed the inside of each one before giving her pussy one long lick from the bottom to the top.

"Damn girl. I wasn't expecting you to taste this fucking good," he moaned before diving back in.

"Fuuuccckkk!" Diamond groaned as she spread her legs apart a little further.

Sliding his hands under her ass cheeks, Quentin palmed it tightly holding her in place so she couldn't run away from the tongue lashing he was giving her. Diamond let out a string of cuss words as she felt an unfamiliar feeling take over her body, causing her legs to shake.

"Ooooo! I'm about to cum!" she shouted at the top of her lungs.

Upon eruption, Diamond's body began to shake as her juices flowed out of her like a faucet. Quentin smiled at her as she panted for dear life. His face was glistening with her juices. Diamond slowly caressed her clit, giving him a show as he undressed. Once he was naked, Quentin's dick was at full attention. Licking her juices from her fingers, Diamond gasped as he roughly thrust his thick dick inside her. Quentin held her legs a part at the ankles, giving her tight wet pussy long deep strokes.

"I can see you weren't lying when you said you ain't fucked nobody in years. This shit feels like virgin pussy," He bit his lip.

"Stop playing in this pussy and fuck me," Diamond moaned staring into his eyes.

Obeying her command, Quentin placed her legs on his shoulder and started pounding away.

"Yeeeessss! Just like that! Get that shit!" Diamond cheered him on.

Diamond dug her nails into his skin as he made her feel every inch of his dick in her stomach. It had been years since Diamond was fucked and she was loving the dick that Quentin was giving her. Squeezing his dick with her pussy, she smirked at the faces he started making. Diamond was enjoying everything she was receiving, but she couldn't hold out much longer.

"You ready for me to cum," he growled.

"No, but I'm about to cum," she moaned.

After a few more deep strokes, Diamond came harder than she did the first time and Quentin released every drop of his seed inside her. They both took a moment to catch their breath before he collapsed next to Diamond.

"That pussy is everything," he chuckled. "If you ever give away my pussy, I think I'll kill ya ass?"

"Oh yeah?" she asked in shock.

"Hell yeah," Quentin answered seriously. "Now I see why you were making a nigga work so hard for that thang," he chuckled.

"I told you this pussy was worth waiting for," Diamond grinned.

"You should stay the night again."

"I would like to, but I don't want to impose on you and Justin," she rolled out of bed. "I overheard y'all talking last night. The weekend is y'all's time to chill and bond and shit. The last thing I wanna do is fuck that up," she replied.

"So I guess I'll be spending time at your crib on the weekends then while the boys are at work."

"Sounds good to me, baby." Diamond walked into the master bathroom and hopped into the shower where Quentin joined her.

They fucked once more before they got dressed and

headed out the door and hopped inside the car. The couple talked the entire drive to her house. Diamond thought that Quentin was going to start acting funny towards her now that he got what he wanted the most from her, but hearing him promise that he was going to keep her and Justin made her feel like Quentin really cared about them, which was good because the feeling was mutual. For the first time in a long time, Diamond felt that she found someone that was all about her and Justin, and even though she couldn't control God's will, she prayed that Quentin wouldn't be taken away from her.

CHAPTER 18

Taj sat in his car that was parked in front of home that he was scheduled to look at in Montgomery County, reading the paper. For the past two weeks, he had been checking every paper on a daily basis looking for a story on Banks' murder, but he didn't find one. Taj was also keeping up with news and neither of the many channels covered a story on a man being gunned down in an ally. The previous day, he drove by the alley to see if the body was still there undiscovered, but when he saw that the alley was empty, Taj had a bitch fit because he knew for a fact that he'd killed Banks. He checked his pulse before and after and the nigga was lifeless. There was no way in hell that he could've survived that, but being as though he was nowhere to be found, Taj had to assume the worst, which was that he really did survive. If he wasn't in the paper or the on the news, Taj figured that he had to be in one of the many hospitals in Philly either recovering or in the morgue, and he hoped it was the second one.

The ringing of his phone interrupted his thoughts and Taj knew that it was his brother calling for an update. He didn't want to answer the phone but Taj knew that he was going to have to let Quentin know the truth.

"Yo bro? What's good with you?" he answered with a sigh.

"Ain't shit man. I'm at the club getting everything ready for tonight. How's everything going with the house hunting?"

"Everything is cool. I'm waiting for the realtor to come meet me at this house in Montgomery County but truthfully, I think I'm just gonna get that house not to far from you. That way if some shit pop off, it won't take me that long to get to you and vice versa," Taj replied before sighing again.

"You aight, man? You doing a lot of sighing over there."

"I got something to tell you man and it'll probably fuck ya day up, but believe me when I tell you that I'm gonna fix this shit."

"T, what the fuck are you talking about?" Quentin asked, confused.

"Banks has not been reported dead or missing. I double checked to make sure that motherfucker was dead and somehow his ass is in the fucking wind. I've been stalking every news paper in the city as well as the news looking for something about his death and nothing has been reported."

"Are you fucking kidding me right now!"

"Q. I told you I'm gonna fix this shit man."

"We'll discuss this shit later. Have you heard anything about a nigga named G?"

"My boys told me that the only nigga in the streets with a G name that they know is a nigga named Garrick. He was released from prison a couple of months ago and jumped right back into the streets like he never left. They told me that he's recruiting niggas from every hood to move work for him, but he's recruiting teenagers between the age of thirteen to nineteen. It's a rumor going around that he's trying to

DIAMOND & BOSS

open up some type of business, but it hasn't been proven to be true yet," Taj answered.

"I wish I had a last name for this nigga so I can look him up, but I'll just have to see what I can find," Quentin sighed. "Have you talked to mom and pops yet?"

"Nah, not yet. They called you?"

"Yeah. They said they want us to fly out and come spend some time with them since they hadn't seen us in a while. I'm thinking about taking Diamond with me when we go so they can meet my lady."

"Your lady?" Taj asked in shock.

"That's right nigga. My lady," Quentin chuckled.

"Well congrats bro. It's about time you stopped fucking around and settled down," he honestly spoke.

"Shut up man. I'll hit you up later, and make sure you swing by auntie's house and see Riko."

"Aight."

Placing the phone in his pocket, Taj placed his hand on his head at the thought of his little cousin getting shot. It pissed him off that Riko wanted to follow in their footsteps of their younger years instead of the path they walking as grown men. He was sure that Quentin told his little ass about the pros and cons of the streets, and the fact that Riko disregarded his words and tried to get involve in the streets anyway frustrated the hell out of Taj, but he hoped that he learned his lesson.

Deciding not to wait for the realtor, Taj headed back to the city to check on the salon. It was the last day of the remodeling project and he needed to do a final walk through to make sure everything was done right. While he was speeding down the expressway, his phone rang and he had a feeling it was his pops calling. When he saw that it was, he smirked.

"Yo pops," he answered, "How are you doing?"

"I'm doing good son," his pops, Quentin Senior replied. "Can't complain. How are things out there?"

"Everything is cool, dad. I was supposed to go look at this house but I changed my mind."

"House?"

"Yeah. I decided to move closer to Philly. I'm gonna get this house that's not too far from Q."

"What about your business? Are you gonna open another building?"

"I plan on keeping my construction company in Baltimore and expanding to Philly or either Jersey. I'm not sure yet."

"Okay," he paused, "What's going on out there in them streets?"

"I'd rather discuss when we see each other. It's too much to discuss on the phone," Taj avoided the question.

"As if I don't already know," his pops spoke sternly. "Just because I'm retired and living on the island doesn't mean that I don't keep tabs on you two. Like I told you before, someone is always watching. You need to learn to cover your tracks better and stop leaving loose ends, Taj, but like you said we'll discuss that when I see you. When exactly will that be?"

"Some time in May," Taj didn't hide his sudden irritation.

"Good. I'll hit you up in a couple days. Take care of yourself, son."

"I will."

Ending the call abruptly, Taj tossed his phone in the passenger seat. As much as he loved his pops, he hated that he still treated him as if he was the same young teenage boy that constantly used to fuck up. It was bad enough that he had two possible failed attempts at killing Banks, but the last thing Taj wanted, was to be ridicule about that shit.

Quentin Senior used to be the biggest kingpin in the city

of Philly back in the day and even though damn near everyone knew who he was an what he did, the people loved him all the same. He wouldn't sell drugs to pregnant women, children under the age of twenty-one or elderly people. Quentin Senior was always giving back to the community and was always trying to encourage young boys not follow in his footsteps and strive to be better than him. The community knew of all the good he did, but they never knew how much blood he actually had on his hands. When Taj and Quentin became of age to be a part of the family business, they went through intense training and the first thing they were taught to do was shoot a gun. They learned about the game whenever their pops felt like teaching it to them. Quentin Senior would wake them up in the middle of the night and give them random quizzes of the product, prices, locations, what to do after they caught a body and how to keep from making the news. When Quentin was twenty, he decided to leave the family business because that wasn't the life he wanted to live, while Taj, on the other hand, had shit on lock in Baltimore until Banks fucked up his meeting. When Taj ended up losing his turf and fighting for his life, his pops wouldn't let him live that shit down for months, and he never missed the opportunity to tell him how much of a fuck up he was over the years. As much as Taj loved the streets, Quentin Senior turned his love for the streets into hate and now that he was out, he didn't have to worry about hearing his mouth as much anymore.

Taj pulled up to the salon and saw some of the stylists standing outside anxious to see what the new salon looked like. Parking in front of the building, a couple of the stylists eyed him seductively, but he didn't pay them any mind. Taj unlocked the front door allowing the stylists to head inside first, and from the way they gasped at the much-needed improvements, he knew that they loved what they saw.

Everything in the salon was brand new from the TV, to the hardwood floors. Taj walked through the salon, checking everything thoroughly. He gave the ladies a few more moments to enjoy the new salon before Taj told him that it was time for them to leave. As he locked the door, the ladies started asking him a million and one questions and he told them to direct all questions to Boss.

Getting back in his car, Taj snatched up his ringing phone when he heard Jordan's ringtone.

"Hey baby," he greeted, getting comfortable behind the wheel.

"Hey. Are you busy?"

"Nah. I'm just leaving the salon. I'm actually about to be on my way to see my lil cousin for a hot minute before I come see you. Wassup?"

"I wanted to wait until you got here, but I can't wait."

"Aight. Say what's on your mind, bae."

"Baby. I'm pregnant."

With the phone to his ear, Taj was at a loss for words.

"Are you still there?"

"Yeah. I'm still here," he spoke getting himself together. "I knew I peeped that you weren't feeling well a few times and I know you've been a little on the tired side, but I never thought you were pregnant."

"You don't sound too happy," Jordan sadly responded.

"Of course, I'm happy Jay. My baby is having my baby and this time, I know it's mine," he grinned.

"That's right, because ain't nobody been hitting this pussy but you," she stated boldly.

"I'll see you when I get home bae, and don't tell Diamond yet. I want us to tell her together."

"Okay. See you when you get here."

The grin on Taj's face remained there as he drove to his aunt's house. He couldn't believe that Jordan was pregnant and he couldn't control his excitement. Even though he had a bad pregnancy experience, Taj didn't have any doubts when it came to Jordan being pregnant with his child. Having a child by the woman you loved was one hell of a feeling, and Taj was going to enjoy it to the fullest.

CHAPTER 19

Since linking up with Garrick, Kamaya had been working around the clock for him looking for an office building for his business and digging up information on Banks. She found plenty of buildings for office and business space for him to check out over the weeks, but Garrick had a problem with every property he went to. The buildings were either too small, too close to the hood, too close to center city or too dirty. Kamaya knew that Garrick had every right to be picky, but he was starting to get on her last nerve with his complaints and demands. She was used to handling complaints and demands, but Garrick could be downright disrespectful and cruel. He was degrading her in some way, shape or form and the only reason why Kamaya continued to work for him was because she didn't have any other option. There were times that she wanted to call Boss and beg for him to hire her back, but Kamaya's pride wouldn't allow her to call him.

After weeks of trying to find information on Banks and coming up empty, Kamaya called in a favor to one of her hacker friends she kept on standby for assignments like this.

She sent over a picture of him and his name and within hours, her hacker friend emailed her an entire file on Banks. Once she printed out all of the documents, Kamaya took her time carefully reading through everything and the information that she found out about him made her mouth drop open. The file contained cell phone records as well as the pictures that he had stored on his cell phone at the time. Kamaya knew that Garrick was going to be kissing the ground she walked on when she gave him the file containing the important documents. Saving the file to her laptop, she put the files in a large envelope before she hopped in the shower and got dressed for the day. Before she headed out of her condo, Kamaya sent Garrick a text letting him know where to meet her, which was in front of the property he was going to visit that day.

Hopping in her car, Kamaya brought it to life, pulled out of the spot and drove into traffic. She nodded her head to the music that played from her phone as she cruised through the downtown streets of Philly. The May weather was starting to warm up and after a freezing cold Winter and Spring, Kamaya was ready for the warm weather. Arriving at the property located on Columbus Boulevard, she parked her car and left it running while she waited for Garrick to come out. Ten minutes later, he came strolling out the front door with the realtor walking in front of him. By the way she was smiling, she either got dicked down something proper, or Garrick spit more game than a little bit to shawty. The realtor waved bye as she headed to her car while Garrick got into the passenger side of her car.

"Let's make this shit quick. I got things to do," he spat annoyed.

Reaching in her back seat, Kamaya dropped the large envelope in his lap.

"That's everything you wanted and then some on Banks."

She watched as Garrick opened the envelope removing the documents. The frown that was displayed on his face instantly turned into the smile of the Grinch when he stole Christmas. By the way he stared at the documents told Kamaya that the wheels were spinning in his head, and Garrick was about to put a devious plan in motion and she knew that nothing good could come from it. Instantly regretting giving him the documents, Kamaya remained silent until he was finished looking through the files. Fifteen minutes later, he stuffed the papers back in the envelope, tossed Kamaya an envelope full of cash then he hopped out the car without saying bye.

"Rude ass motherfucker," she shook her head and drove off.

Kamaya ran a few errands before returning home. Her roommate, Ebony, was at work so she had the condo to herself until later on that night. Changing her clothes, she made herself something to eat and flopped down on the couch and began to binge watch 'Balck Ink Crew Chicago'. As she thought about Garrick and his rude ass behavior, Kamaya decided to give her hacker friend his name and picture. Although she had history with him already, Kamaya needed some type of leverage on him in case he decided to jump stupid and do some fly shit. She wasn't going to keep tolerating disrespect from him, and she needed to use it against him to keep him in line.

As she waited for the file to come through, her phone began to ring and she answered it.

"Hey Eb. What's good?"

"Bitch, you need to stop working for Garrick," she whispered. "That nigga is bat shit crazy. I know you're not involved in his street activities but you need to leave him alone altogether," Ebony rambled.

"Girl what the fuck are you talking about? What's going on?"

"That nigga is out here recruiting kids to sell drugs for him and the kids who don't agree, he has the kids that are riding with him killing the kids and their family members. I heard he shot Boss's lil cousin because Riko wouldn't kill Boss or his homie. I always knew that Garrick was a sick son of bitch, but he's taking that shit to a new level. You gotta leave him alone, Maya. I'm serious."

The news that was just relayed to her had Kamaya's heart beating rapidly.

"Thanks for the heads up. We'll talk when you get home."

She hung up on her friend and paced the floor. Kamaya knew that Garrick was into the street shit again, but he didn't know that he was recruiting kids to be a part of his operation. Learning that Garrick shot Boss's little cousin made her feel some type of way, and she knew that Boss was probably looking to get even. When the file came through, Kamaya sat in front her on her laptop, biting her fingernails. She didn't know if she should send the file to Boss or not but because of the love she still had for him, she emailed him the file without reading it. Kamaya knew that she probably had just signed Garrick's death certificate, but she really didn't give a fuck. Garrick needed to be stopped and she knew that Boss and Taj were the men who could stop him.

CHAPTER 20

Since the club opened nearly two weeks of ago, Quentin had been busier than ever with the daily operations. After hiring a manager to take over and a club promoter, he was able to kick back for a little bit and focus on his upcoming trip to the Bahamas where their parents resided. Quentin hadn't seen his parents in two years and their conversations were far and few in between. Since their father retired from the streets, their parents spent a year traveling the world and decided to spend the remainder of their lives in the Bahamas. Although Quentin was certain that he was going to see his parents, he couldn't help the uneasy feeling that came over him. The last conversation he had with his parents, everything seemed cool when he was talking to his pops, but his mother was a different story. She seemed as if she was holding back from telling him something important. He didn't know if it was because she was around their father or she just wasn't ready to reveal what she'd been holding on to. Whatever the reason, it made him wonder what it was that his mother had to say.

When Friday approached, Quentin was double parked

outside of Gratz High School, waiting for the boys to get out. It was Riko's first week back at school and he called him everyday to see if he was having problems. Riko informed him that the boys he was hanging with looked like they had seen a ghost when they saw him in school that Monday. The dope boys hadn't given him any problems. Just stares. Quentin told him that he would be there to pick him up every day to make sure he got to work safely. When the bell rang, he got out the truck and leaned up against it. The students poured out of the set of double doors and when he spotted Justin and Riko, he saw two dudes push them and before he could even blink, the four boys were rumbling. The students stopped walking and gathered around in a circle. Quentin bullied his way through the crowd and pulled the rivals away from Justin and Riko, tossing them to the ground.

The boys jumped to their feet, but Quentin stood in front of them.

"Move the fuck out the way!" One of the boys yelled.

"Look youugin'. You done already got ya ass whooped. Take ya L on the chin and leave it alone," he spoke calmly.

Turning to walk away, the loud mouth boy ran up on Quentin but before he could touch him, he quickly turned around and gripped the boy up by his throat lifting him off his feet.

"I don't fight kids youngin'. I fight adults. If you got a problem tell ya pops, uncle or old head to come holla at me because the next time you run up on me, it ain't gonna be a good look for ya dumb ass," Quentin dropped the little boy on the ground and walked off with Riko and Justin in front of him.

Quentin heard the kids laughing at the boy that got clowned as they hopped in the truck and drove off.

"Damn, Q. Ya ass gonna be all over World Star for that shit," Riko joked from the front seat.

"I don't give a fuck. Lil niggas these days is outta pocket," Quentin scoffed. "I shoulda whooped his ass with my belt."

"I gotta hand it to you, Jus. You nice with them hands, man. I didn't think you had it in ya. You know they say pretty boys can't fight," Riko teased.

"Those rules don't apply to me. I'm far from a bitch," Justin huffed. "Them motherfukers been itching for that ass whooping all week. Pussy ass niggas."

"Whoa Justin," Quentin quickly glanced in the backseat. "I thought Riko was the only one that cussed."

"Please. When Jus gets angry, he turns into a different nigga," Ricko chuckled.

Quentin glanced in the backseat again and saw Justin staring out the window, still angry. Being as though he understood his frustration, he decided to let him be. Quentin knew what it was like for boys like Justin who was the do-good type. Niggas tended to pick with them because they think the good kids are soft, but as Justin proved, not all of them are sweet.

Arriving at the clothing store, Quentin parked in the spot, hopped out and headed inside. The boys went to the back to change while he kept walking to his office. Quentin sat behind his desk powering up his iMac. Before he could he could do anything, there was a knock on the door. When he saw it was Diamond, he stood to his feet to greet her. They embraced each other, and Quentin didn't miss the opportunity to grab her ass.

"Were Justin and Riko in a fight," she asked frantically, breaking their embrace.

"A fight did pop off as soon as they walked outta school, but they held their own before I broke it up."

"Got damn it," she sighed. "Now Justin's gonna have an

attitude all damn weekend. When he gets mad, he doesn't settle down for days."

"Well you let me worry about that, Diamond. That's why he has me, so I can help him with these types of issues."

"You're right," she smiled. "I'm not gonna stay long. I just wanted to stop by and see you and tell you thank you for the money you left on top of my bills," Diamond grinned.

"Don't sweat that," he licked his lips with his hands around her waist, "You know I gotta make sure my girl is taken care of. Even if her strong, independent ass says she doesn't need it." Quentin smacked her lightly on the ass, making her blush.

"Well thank you, baby. I appreciate you," Diamond kissed his lips. "I gotta go. Jordan is in the car and we're going to look at baby stuff and to shop for our trip to the Bahamas."

"Damn. She's going baby shopping already?" he chuckled.

"Yes," she giggled, "Jordan is so excited about this baby. That's all she ever talks about now."

"Aight. Well hurry up and get on outta here before I bend you over my desk. I don't know why you came in here with all that ass in a sun dress," he bit his lip.

"Bye baby," she pecked his lips before switching out of his office.

Watching her ass jiggle in that dress made his dick hard as fuck. Quentin never missed the opportunity to dick his baby down and the more they had sex, the weaker they became for each other. No woman had ever made him feel the way that Diamond did and even though he had the means to take care of her, she still wanted to do for herself and that's what he loved about her. Most chicks would have become lazy or probably quit their jobs if they had a boss to support them, but Diamond still got up for work every morning and went to school at night. She even cooked for Boss when he wanted to go out and cleaned up his place when she went over there.

Quentin informed her that he had a cleaning service come to his house once a week to clean, but she insisted on doing it, and that was sexy as fuck to him.

He sat behind his desk and began checking his emails. Quentin tried to check his email on a daily basis but no matter how often he cleared them, his inbox was always full. He went through his business emails and forwarded most of them to the manager over at the club so he could respond to the birthday inquires, and erased the rest because they were junk mail. Switching over to his personal account, Quentin scanned through the emails to see if it was anything important, and came across an email from Kamaya, marked urgent. He hadn't spoken to her in weeks and although she no longer worked for him, Quentin still trusted her judgement when it came to certain things. Clicking the email, he read the text.

"I heard about what happened to your cousin and thought you might need this."

He saw the attachment with Garrick's name on it. He quickly clicked the link and the attachment opened. Quentin was intrigued with the information that he was finding out, but the more he learned about Garrick Richardson, the angrier he became. By the time he reached the end of the file, all Quentin could do was stare at the screen with his mouth gapped open. After taking a few moments to register the information he'd just read, he snatched up his phone, calling his brother.

"Wassup Q?"

"I need you to meet me at the clothing store, and quick. You're not gonna believe the shit I just found out."

CHAPTER 21

"**G**irl, I can't believe that we're really going to the Bahamas," Diamond squealed as she talked to Jordan on FaceTime. "But I am a bit nervous about meeting their parents, though."

"Girl, you're not alone," Jay agreed. "The last time I met a dude's mom, I was getting ready to knock her damn head off for calling me a ho," she rolled her eyes.

"I remember that," Diamond chuckled. "Some of these parents be in the way. Especially the moms. They're so over protective of their sons. I remember when I met Damien's mom. She purposely kept pronouncing my name wrong on purpose. I kept telling her my name is Diamond and she kept calling Simon, Simone, Dias and Desmond. She mispronounced my name for the first year of our relationship," she spat.

"Yeah. She had a real issue with you. Reminds me of the mother from *Think Like A Man* when the mama's boy was dating the single mama," Jordan laughed. "If I have a son, I'm gonna try not to be like that but being as though this is my first, I already know this baby is going to be spoiled to pieces," she grinned. "I still can't believe I'm pregnant."

"Shit. I can! As much fucking you said y'all be doing, it was only a matter of time child," Diamond laughed.

"Shut up D," Jay smirked. "Cause at the rate y'all going, you're gonna be the next one to pop up pregnant," she teased.

"Bitch, don't put that curse on me! I got one more semester of school until I get my Master's then after that, I might consider having kids."

"I still can't believe that you bagged Quentin Marks, the biggest play boy of Philly. Not only did you bag him but you got that nigga being faithful and everything. I thought that nigga was gonna try at least once to see if you were all talk like most niggas do, but he hasn't and I don't think he will. I think he loves you, Diamond."

"You really think so?"

"Fuck yeah! He wouldn't be acting the way he does if he didn't."

Diamond couldn't help but smile as she thought about how well her relationship with Quentin was going. She was in disbelief herself about being Quentin's girlfriend. Diamond had been fighting her feelings for him since the first time they made love because she didn't want to get too attached to him, but the more time they spent together, the more she fell in love with him. Quentin had put his arrogance and pride to the side and showed her the loving, caring and thoughtful side of him. Quentin always checked on her throughout the day; he made sure that she was keeping up with her school work and he even rubbed Diamond's feet after a long day of work. Diamond wanted to tell Quentin how she felt about him and that she loved him, but every time she was around him, she couldn't find the words.

"I hope you're right Jay, because I'm gonna feel like a fool if I tell Q I love him and he doesn't say it back."

"Oh my God Diamond! Did you just say you loved Q?" Jordan gasped.

"Yes I did," she blushed.

"Giirrll, I'm so happy for you. After years of not being in a relationship, you put yourself out there and found love again after vowing that you would never date again," her eyes watered.

"Well, I have you to thank you for that. If it wasn't for you encouraging me to move on with my life, I would still be without a man and holding onto memories of my ex."

"Anytime, girl."

The ladies laughed and talked while they packed their suitcases for their trip. When Diamond learned that Taj was buying a house in the same cul-de-sac as Quentin and that they were going to be moving in together when all the paperwork was done, she almost passed out from the news. She was so happy that things were going so well for her friend and Jordan deserved all that happiness in the world. Once they were finished packing, it was time for Jordan to take her nap and Diamond told her that she would talk to her later.

Placing her suitcase in the closet, she snatched her phone off the bed before walking into the living room and turning on the TV. *'What's Love Got To Do With It'*, one of her favorite movies, was playing on BET and it was just coming on. Diamond scurried to the kitchen, heated up some of the leftover fried chicken and mashed potatoes she'd made the night before, poured herself a tall glass of wine and got comfortable on the couch. As she ate her food, Diamond was glued to the TV like it was her first time seeing the movie.

In the middle of the of the movie, someone knocked on her door, interrupting her. Hoping that they would go away, she ignored it but that didn't stop the person from knocking. Diamond jumped up from the couch marching over to the door. She looked through the peep hole and was shocked when she saw who was on the other side. Unlocking the door, Diamond hesitated before opening it.

"Diamond," the girl smiled.

"Danisha? What…what are you doing here?"

"I needed to talk to you. May I come in?"

Moving to the side, Diamond let her come in and closed the door behind her. Danisha walked over to the couch and Diamond joined her, turning off the TV.

"What do you need to talk to me about?"

"I'm here about my brother," she sighed.

"Damien?" she raised an eyebrow. "What about your brother? He's been gone for three years now."

"No. He hasn't," Danisha corrected her.

"Say what now?" Diamond asked with an attitude.

"I know my mother told you that he was killed by a drunk driver and that there wouldn't be a funeral because he was cremated, but she lied," she confessed.

"What the fuck you mean she lied!" Diamond jumped up from the couch.

"My mother didn't like the idea of the two of you getting married. So she told him that if he married you that she would disown Damien as her son. He was willing to take that chance of losing the relationship with our mom but when he thought about you and Justin, he felt as though that he wouldn't be able to take care of y'all. He wasn't man enough to tell you that he couldn't be engaged to you anymore, so he left without saying a word. My mom told you that he died so you would stop calling," Danisha explained.

"I can't believe this shit!" she began pacing the floor, "So you mean that motherfucker has been alive all this time, and he didn't reach out to me at all?"

"Damien hasn't kept in contact with anyone for years. He left Philly a couple of weeks after he proposed to you but he didn't tell anyone where he was going. I knew that he was alive for all these years because of the twin instinct we have, but for a month, I've been feeling like Damien is hurt or in danger and I need your help finding him, Diamond."

Diamond's blood pressure was through the roof as she continued to pace the floor. She was so angry that she began to cry. She couldn't believe that Damien's fraternal twin came in and dropped that bomb on her. For years, Diamond suffered from a broken heart because she thought Damien, the man she was once going to marry, was dead, but to learn that he'd been walking the face of the earth all this time and he hadn't reached out to her at all over the years pissed her smooth the fuck off. It had taken years for her to get over him and she was determined not to open that door again, but knowing that Damien was alive, a part of her wanted to know if it was true or not.

"So, Diamond? Are you gonna help me or not?"

CHAPTER 22

The beeping noises that sounded around him made Bashir began to steer in his sleep. Slowly opening his eyes, he thought that he was in heaven because of the bright light the shined above his head, but when Bashir's vision cleared, he realized that he was in the hospital. The room was silent with the exception of the monitor. He tried to recall when or how he arrived at the hospital but came up clueless. Bashir slowly sat up in the hospital bed, grabbing the pitcher off the bed table and began drinking straight out of it. His mouth was beyond dry and he needed to wet his whistle. Damn near emptying the pitcher, Bashir placed it back on the table. Noticing his cell phone, he grabbed it off the table and tried to turn it on, but the battery was too low. Thoughts of his family entered his mind and he needed to know what the hell was going on with him. He went to reach for the room phone and froze when he heard the door open.

"Well, hello there, Mr. Phillips," a light skinned CNA entered his room. "I'm glad you're finally awake. Some of us were starting to believe that you weren't going to make it," she spoke sadly.

"What happened? How did I get here?" Bashir looked at her strangely.

"I was told that your brother brought you in. He said that you were the victim of a shooting you and you had multiple gunshot wounds. They performed emergency surgery and they were able to remove the bullets from your body, but you slipped into a coma, and you've been in one for a nearly two months now; but you brother was here everyday to check on you," she smiled.

Bashir was stunned by the information he'd just received and was confused to hear about his so-called brother, because he didn't have one.

"How are you feeling, Mr. Phillips?"

"I'm aight I guess," he shrugged. "I'd be better if I could remember what happened to me."

"Now that's a question I can't answer for you, but maybe your brother can. He stepped out for a minute, but I'll tell him that you're woke. If you need anything, just hit the call button. My name is Virginia," she grinned before leaving the room.

Bashir grabbed the room phone, dialing Morgan's number and when the message that the number he was dialing was no longer in service, he hung the phone up, tossing his head back in frustration. A few minutes later, the room door opened again and this time a man about his height entered. Bashir locked eyes with the stranger as he walked across the room and sat in the chair that was placed on the right side of his bed. They stared at each other a moment longer before the stranger spoke.

"I was surprised to hear that you were woke. I was starting to think that you weren't going to pull through," he spoke solemnly.

"I'm assuming that you're my brother and you brought me?" Bashir continued to grill him.

"Yeah, I did, and I would like a little appreciation for my act of good will."

"We'll discuss your act of good will after you refresh my memory of what happened to me?"

"I don't know the whole story, but I've been keeping tabs on you for weeks now. Someone mentioned your name to me and said that you used to rob kingpins and connect deals back in the day, and I decided that you were someone I needed on my team. The day that you were gunned down in the alley, I saw that you were following Boss, but someone was following you, too. They left ya ass for dead in that alley, but I found you and rushed you here. You slipped into a coma during surgery and you're just now waking up. I'm sure Virginia told you everything else."

Hearing the stranger talk about the day of his shooting helped Bashir remember all that happened that day. Boss had fired him and he was going to kill him for doing so, and Morgan cussed him out for lying to Boss and fucking up the opportunity of a life time. He remembered following Boss to club, but he took the back way and that's when he was shot down in the alley.

"I remember now," he groaned, "Thank you for bringing me here."

"No problem brother," the stranger smirked.

"But what I don't understand is why you saved me? You don't know shit about me and we've never crossed paths. So what do you want from me?"

"I saved you because I feel as though you would be a good addition to my team. I need a business partner for a project I'm trying to launch as well as help me take over the streets. I've heard about your ruthless, savage behavior and I need someone like you on my team," He beamed.

"I don't mind being your business partner, but I don't have a history of being in the streets," Bashir lied.

The stranger stood to his feet as he chuckled.

"Oh, Banks. You may have been able to lie to the people in your life for all these years but the one thing you can never do, is lie to me. Now, if we're gonna be in business together, I need you to be straight forward with me."

Bashir gave the stranger the side eye as he walked back and forth in front of the window. He didn't know who he was or how he knew that he was lying, but he needed to not make the same mistake twice like he'd done with Boss.

"Aight," he sighed. "Yes I was involved in the streets. I murked niggas in multiple states for large amounts of bread and I got a lot of blood on my hands. The niggas that shot me, I think it was somebody I robbed from my past."

"Now we're getting somewhere," he grinned. "Now your fiancée, does she know that she's not the only woman you've been in love with?"

"What?"

"Does Morgan know that you were in love with another woman before her?" He asked again.

"Morgan is the only person I've been with exclusively," Bashir answered sternly.

"Tsk, tsk, tsk. There you go lying again, Banks."

Bashir was tired of playing nice with the unknown stranger. He was pissing him off with the information he was reciting and wanted to know what the fuck he thought he knew about him.

"I'm tired of you saying that I'm lying, and you don't even know shit about me to verify the shit you are spitting," he roared angrily.

"Oh, I know everything I need to know about you, Damien Moore," he replied with a devilish grin.

Hearing his government name caused Bashir to tense up immediately. No one that he was affiliated with knew who he really was, and he preferred it that way. When Bashir was almost killed in his last robbery, he laid low, changed his name and transformed into a new man as a way of leaving his old life behind and creating a new one. Bashir knew shit was real when he was gunned down in the alley, but now that a complete stranger had his true identity, he didn't know what to expect.

"Who the fuck are you, and how did you find that out?"

"I'm sure you remember Kamaya. The bougie bitch that used to be Boss's business partner?"

"Used to?"

"Yeah. She works for me now. I told her to find out some info about you and she gave me a thick ass file on you, Damien. You've had quite a life. You were a nerd that turned gangsta, huh?"

"Yeah. Something like that," he mumbled.

"Let me stop fucking with you and give the real." The stranger went back over to the chair and sat down. "I do want you to be my partner, but I also would like you to help me take out our common enemy."

"Boss?"

"That's right, and everyone that's connected to him in any way, shape or form. Are you with me?"

"Before I agree to anything, I need a name."

"My name is Garrick and we have more in common than you think, but we'll get into that later. So do we have a deal?"

"Hell yeah," Bashir answered with an extended hand.

"Before we shake on this, there's one more thing I have to tell you. When I say that you have to kill everyone that's connected to Boss, I mean everyone. Including his girl, which is someone that's close to you."

"Boss is fucking Morgan?" He leaned forward.

"No. Not Morgan.... Diamond," Garrick smirked, "and her brother Justin."

Bashir felt like the room was at a stand still. After hearing

Diamond's and Justin's names it caused him to go into a trance. Bashir spent plenty of nights trying to erase Diamond from his memory, but he never could and even though he was engaged to Morgan and they shared a child together, Bashir didn't love her the way that he loved Diamond. Diamond was the only woman he wanted and the fact that he had to leave her and Justin behind to keep them from getting hurt for the many lives he took damn near killed him. When he decided to change his identity, the first-person Bashir wanted to call was Diamond, but he figured that she had moved on since so much time had passed, and he didn't want to interrupt her life. Hearing that she was dating Boss tore his heart in two and since he agreed to help Garrick kill Boss, Bashir didn't know if he could kill the woman he stilled loved, and her brother.

"So what do you say, Damien? Are you riding with me or what?"

TO BE CONTINUED...

AUTHOR'S NOTES

Thank you for taking the time to read Diamond & Boss: A Hood Love Story and I hope you enjoyed reading this book as much as I enjoyed writing it. I would like to thank all of the readers who have supported my work over the years. I appreciate each and every one of y'all! If this is your first time reading a novel from me, I hope you enjoyed this book enough to check out the rest of my catalog.